Evernight Publishing

www.evernightpublishing.com

Copyright© 2015

Jessica Jayne

Editors: JS Cook, Brieanna Robertson

Cover Artist: Sour Cherry Designs

Packet Design: Jay Aheer

ISBN: 978-1-77233-301-5

ALL RIGHTS RESERVED

TAKING ADVANTAGE

DEDICATION

Always to my husband for his support and love.

To Jenika - Thanks so much for your thoughts and insight in helping me to not only name this book but also this series! You rock!

TAKING ADVANTAGE

BOARD STIFF

Taking Advantage, 1

Jessica Jayne

Copyright © 2013

Chapter One

"Where's today's agenda?" John Dorsey asked as he sat down in one of the many black leather chairs in the board room. He reached for the stainless steel coffee carafe and poured the dark brown liquid into his white porcelain coffee mug. Despite having had a cup of coffee on the way into the office, John usually needed about a carafe of coffee to make it through a board meeting day. He wasn't used to sitting so many hours at a time. Heading up Dorsey Construction meant he was in the field assisting his construction managers with various projects. Sitting in a chair for six to eight hours listening to presentations on company matters, discussing and approving company budgets and sorting through the financials of Advantage Insurance Company made for long days. John was honored to be asked to sit on the board of directors a year ago. He was the youngest member of the board at thirty-five, and it was good for his business to have such a prestigious role with one of the Tampa Bay area's best known companies. Luckily, the board only met once a quarter.

"Here you go, Mr. Dorsey," Suzie McCormick said with a smile. She handed him a blue folder that he knew contained the day's agenda and the most current quarter's financials. All of the presentations could be seen on the individual iPads at each seat.

"Thank you, Suzie," he said. He took the folder from her hands and set in front of him on the mahogany table. Suzie stood there smiling at him for a few seconds before turning around, flipping her long blonde hair over her shoulder and walking around the table to place the same blue folder at each seat. John watched as she finished up and left the board room for her desk in the executive suite, which was just outside of the boardroom.

Suzie was attractive, albeit a little on the skinny side, at least for John. Suzie was tall, probably 5'10" without heels, and slender. He preferred his women with a little meat on their bones. He loved women with curves. Women were supposed to be soft. Suzie had made it known that she was attracted to John. She flirted with him relentlessly every meeting. A few of the other board members teased him. They encouraged him to ask her out or at the very least, "take her for a ride" they'd say. Even Suzie's boss, Michael Herron, the CEO of Advantage, would occasionally joke with him about her excitement on board week.

"She's got the hots for you, Dorsey," Mark Olson said, walking up to John and extending his hand. Mark was the next youngest member of the board at forty. He had recently divorced his wife of fifteen years. Rumor was that he had had a mid-life crisis and his wife couldn't deal with it. John wasn't positive of Mark's real story, and he never really felt comfortable enough asking him. But Mark was now hot-to-trot for any woman that was good-looking and younger than thirty. "You should really consider it. If she showed me half the attention she shows you, I'd be all over it." He shook John's hand before taking a seat next to John and pouring himself a cup of coffee.

"Knock it off, Mark," John said with a little laugh. "You look a little tired. Late night?" He figured a change of subject would be good before the rest of the directors took their seats, and Mark did look a little tired.

"You could say that," Mark said with a wink. He brought his coffee mug to his lips and took a sip. "I met a hot little number last weekend down at the Beach Club. I've had a few later nights than I'm used to." He chuckled.

"Gentlemen," Phillip Barker said, walking into the room in his crisp khaki pants and green country club polo shirt. All the other board members wore dress slacks and a button down shirt, but Phillip didn't make it mandatory. He was retired and took the position he only wore suits to weddings and funerals now. He took his seat at the head of the long table as chairman of the board. John respected Phil, who had also been in the construction business for much of his life. He gave John a lot of great advice on the trade after he took over the company from his father, John Sr., and John appreciated the man's insight.

"Phil," John said, nodding his head in the direction of Phil. The rest of the board members filtered in. There were six outside directors and Michael Herron, the CEO, sat as the sole inside director on the board. Everyone grabbed their seats and poured coffee.

"Bagel? Scone? We have cinnamon and cherry," Suzie said, walking in with a basket full of bagels and pastries. She offered the basket to John first. He smiled and pulled a cinnamon scone from the basket and placed it on a napkin in front of him.

"Thanks, Suzie," he said kindly.

"Any time, Mr. Dorsey," she said sweetly. The other men chuckled as she made her way around the table to offer the treats to them before placing the basket in the center of the table. Before exiting the room and closing the door behind her, she looked over her shoulder and smiled at John. He felt everyone's gaze on him when the door finally clicked shut.

"What?" he asked, feeling a little embarrassed by all the attention. It wasn't that John wasn't used to attention. He was. Women hit on him all the time. And from time to time, he would flirt back. Maybe ask them out to dinner. Sometimes it would lead to sex at their place… only their place, so he could easily escape when it was over. But since Shayna, John shut himself off from anything other than sex. Finding his ex-fiancée in bed with his best friend left a bad taste in his mouth for relationships. They were a waste of time. He kept telling himself he wanted nothing beyond the desire to satisfy his sexual needs and have a little companionship for an evening. Even though most of his friends had settled down… a few of them on their second marriages, he wasn't interested in taking that route. It was nothing but trouble.

"Dorsey, we have to tease you," Andy Price snickered. "Perhaps we're all just jealous that she's only got eyes for you."

"Can we get started?" John asked, slightly annoyed. Maybe he should just take Suzie out and shut them all up. It had been a couple weeks since he'd been on a "date." The thing was, he would have to see her every quarter for board meetings, and he knew it would never go beyond a date or two. *Forget that idea!* He pulled out the agenda from his blue folder and set it in front of him. "Based on the agenda, it may be a long day."

"Sure thing, Dorsey," Phil said with a smile. "Let's call this meeting to order."

Chapter Two

Elizabeth Wright's palms were sweating. Her boss, Corbin Shaw, the general counsel for Advantage Insurance Company asked her to do the presentation to the board of directors on the big construction defect case that would likely plague the company for the next couple years. Advantage insured three of the twenty defendants in the lawsuit. There were multiple construction issues with a beachfront condominium project, and since her arrival at Advantage three months ago, Elizabeth had been following the case closely. The impact of the lawsuit could cost Advantage millions in defense costs, not to mention what the company may have to pay out if found liable. She understood Corbin's request for her to discuss the case because she was the most knowledgeable about the case, but that didn't make it any less nerve-racking.

"Liz, you will do fine," Corbin said, sitting next to her on the leather couch just outside the board room. She held one piece of paper in her hand that had a short outline of the players in the case. Everything else was pretty well set in her head.

"I know," she whispered. She ran a hand through her long auburn hair. "I know this case like the back of my hand." And she had done her homework. Last night, she had studied the Advantage annual statement from last year and familiarized herself with each of the board members. She had already met Michael Herron, Advantage's CEO, as he was a regular visitor to the Legal Department to meet with Corbin. But the other members were not as well-known to her. In reviewing their bios, she noted that the board consisted of only men... three that were of her father's age or older. But there were three board members that were considerably younger than the others… John Dorsey, Mark Olson and Gregory Snow. She found it interesting that they were appointed members of the board of directors at such young ages. All were tops in their career paths, at least according to her research on LinkedIn and Google. But John Dorsey caught her attention the most. There was something about the look in his eyes in his bio picture that intrigued Elizabeth. Not to mention, he was very easy on the eyes.

"I wouldn't have asked you to do it if I didn't have the utmost faith in you," Corbin said, smiling at her. Corbin was a good guy. He was in his late fifties with dark brown hair that was streaked with gray. He was married with two children in college. As far as bosses went, Elizabeth considered herself quite lucky. She had worked five years in a large law firm right out of law school and she worked her ass off. She applied for the corporate counsel position at Advantage because she was tired of working the ridiculously long billable hours. Her social life had been non-existent for the five years she slaved away at Barnes and Simon. She held high hopes that she could gain her life back as in-house counsel. She was thirty-one. She wanted to get married someday… have a family.

She had more than enough experience to be an asset to a company like Advantage. She had done nothing but handle insurance defense cases at her firm. In fact, she had become quite a commodity at the firm for her aggressiveness in the courtroom. So, when Corbin got her resume for the open position, he immediately asked her in for an interview. He basically hired her on the spot. Her salary went down a bit from her law firm salary, but she hoped her life would go up.

"Corbin." The board room door opened slightly and Phillip Barker poked his head around the corner.

Elizabeth recognized him from his bio photograph in the annual statement. This made her grateful that she did her research. "You ready?"

"Yes, Phil, we're ready," Corbin said, standing from the couch and straightening out his suit jacket.

"Come on in," Phil said, opening the door wide. Elizabeth stood up from the couch and straightened out her taupe skirt and jacket before walking through the door into a board room full of men. She followed Corbin to the front of the room.

"Gentlemen, I'd like to introduce Elizabeth Wright. She is one of our corporate counsel here in Advantage's legal department. We stole her from Barnes and Simon in Tampa, and we are more than thrilled to have her with us. She's been following the beachfront condo construction defect case for us for the last three months and has worked closely with the claims adjusters to get a better understanding of the problems with the building, should there be any coverage issues that will need to be raised under the policies. I thought it would be best if she presented the case to you since she has the most first-hand knowledge of how it may play out for Advantage and its insureds."

"Thank you, Corbin," Elizabeth said, confidently. "And thank you, gentlemen, for allowing me to be here today to talk to you about this case." She lifted her head to scan the room. When her gaze fell on the extremely good-looking man sitting across the table from her, she almost fell to her knees on the spot. *Holy shit! John Dorsey's bio picture did **not** do him justice...at all!* He was gorgeous...lightly tanned skin, dark brown hair, hazel eyes that appeared almost golden. By the way his white button down shirt conformed to his biceps, shoulders and chest, he barely hid his well-sculpted body underneath. *Good God*! And he was staring at her! His gaze skimmed over her body like he was slowly removing her clothes. The heat from his gaze made her feel naked standing there, and her skin flushed when she noticed John adjust his sitting position. His eyes were smoldering. Elizabeth felt everyone else's gaze on her, and that brought her back to the reality of her situation. She had a presentation to give. She tore her gaze from John's. She was always her best under pressure, and clearly, the pressure was on now. She cleared her throat. "As you know, Advantage has three insureds involved in the construction of this project, so there is a good possibility that Advantage's financials may be affected by this case at some point." Elizabeth carried on with her presentation, making damn sure her gaze never wandered over to John Dorsey. She felt the heat of his stare, as if he were tempting her… coaxing her to look at him. But she knew if she looked into his golden eyes again, she'd stumble with the end of her presentation, and she couldn't have that. So, she avoided him. After wrapping up her presentation, Corbin stepped up to the table next to her.

"Do you have any questions for us?" he asked politely.

"When do we suspect we will have a full understanding of the construction issues so that we will know the extent of liability of the individual insureds?" one of the board members Elizabeth recognized as Gregory Snow asked. She knew he was a big corporate law attorney for a large firm in St. Petersburg, Florida.

"Forensic engineers have begun the testing and analysis of the building and common areas," Elizabeth replied. "All defendants agreed to one forensic engineering company to run the tests. It's much cheaper for the defendants if they all pitch in on the cost of this expert and just discuss the results at that point. We expect them to be completed with their report within the next month. At that point, we will have a better understanding of the true defects." Gregory nodded and smiled at her warmly.

"Thanks, Elizabeth," Phil said. "We expect to have you back next quarter to give us an update on the expert report. Great presentation." Phillip smiled at her. Elizabeth felt great. The chairman of the board was pleased with her presentation despite the few seconds she lost her head mentally devouring John Dorsey. She released a breath she didn't even know she had been holding.

"You're welcome, sir," Elizabeth replied, almost breathless. She heard a quiet rumble come from across the table and her gaze shifted to the sound. *Did anyone else hear it?* The other members appeared to be carrying on conversations, but John's gaze was on her. He shifted in his chair again and he bit down on his lower lip. A warmth spread throughout her body and settled between her legs. She was certain that if she slid her hand under her skirt to her panties, she would find them wet. This man made her pussy wet with just a look. It had been a few months since she had had sex, but this guy put her body in overdrive without even touching her. Not that he was going to touch her. *Good Lord!* She was getting carried away. She needed to get out of here.

Corbin thanked the officers and headed out of the board room. Elizabeth followed close behind him, grateful to escape John's heated stare. Once outside, she took a deep breath.

"You did great in there, Liz," Corbin said, patting her on the back. "I get the feeling they are going to want you to give more presentations." He winked at her as they walked back to their department on the second floor.

Chapter Three

John watched as she walked out of the board room. His cock was as hard as a rock. He had to adjust himself twice during her presentation. He'd never been in the presence of a woman that made him instantly hard. She walked into the room with her thick auburn hair flowing over her shoulders. Her green eyes twinkling. Her skirt hugging her in all the right places. *Damn!* And she was smart. Every word out of her mouth made him inconceivably harder. Normally on a case like this, he would have had a ton of questions for Corbin. Being in the construction industry, John was so familiar with all trades that he was usually good with these discussions. But his brain short-circuited. All he could think about was sliding above Elizabeth's sexy body and sinking deep inside it. He had to have her! He didn't care what he had to do to get her and he didn't care who, if anyone, stood in his way.

"Dorsey, we expected you to have some questions," Mark said with a small laugh. "Did Ms. Wright distract you? I'll admit she distracted me." John shot Mark a sharp look. That horny fucker had better not even think about approaching her.

"I want to wait until we have the expert report. At this point, it's just a finger-pointing game," John said, trying to act nonchalant despite having his first ever boner during a board meeting.

"I agree with John," Phil said. "These construction defect cases are usually a mess. Next quarter, we should have a better feel of where our insureds stand. Let's take a break. Lunch should be here shortly." Everyone got up from their seats and stretched, except for John. Once he thought he had his hard-on under control, he got up and walked over to Suzie's desk.

Her blue eyes lit up like a Christmas tree as he stood in front of her.

"Mr. Dorsey, can I help you?" she asked eagerly. Too eagerly. A smile spread across her face. He knew his question would wipe that huge smile from her lips.

"Yes, Suzie, you can help me," he said, trying to be as sweet as possible. He tried to keep the desire out of his voice, but the prospect of seeing Elizabeth again made it impossible. "Can you point me in the direction of Elizabeth Wright's office?" he asked. He watched as the smile slipped from her lips and her blue eyes turned down. The look on her face told him she knew exactly why he wanted to find Elizabeth.

"You'll need to go down to the second floor," she said shortly. "Legal is on the north end of the building." She stood up from her desk and walked briskly away from him, without doing her signature over-the-shoulder look at him. He didn't want to hurt her feelings. She was a nice woman, but he had never expressed any interest in her beyond a friendly acquaintance. He wasn't attracted to Suzie. Not much he could do about it. But Elizabeth… she had sparked something in him he had never experienced before… a desire… a need. Even Shayla hadn't gotten under his skin like Elizabeth had.

John took the escalator down to the second floor and easily found the legal department. Despite being on the board of directors for about a year, John didn't know most of the employees in the company. He knew most of the officers that presented to the board regularly. And he had bumped into several employees at the company Christmas party last year, but he had had a few drinks and couldn't guarantee he could recall most of their names.

"Mr. Dorsey," a woman greeted him upon his walking through the legal department doors. She sat outside what he figured was Corbin's office based on its size.

"Hi," John said. He held out his hand to her. "Please call me John."

"Welcome to legal, John. I'm Roni… Corbin's executive assistant. Can I help you?" She shook his hand gently. Roni's brown hair was cut short and cropped around her delicate face and her light brown eyes were gentle. He figured she was probably in her early fifties.

"Yes, Roni, I'm looking for Elizabeth's office." He smiled at her, and he watched as a soft smile spread across her face.

"Certainly. Last door on the left," she said, pointing down the short hallway. John strode quietly down the hallway towards the last door. He peeked in the open doorway. She was sitting at her L-shaped desk facing the window, typing away on her computer. He watched her for a few seconds. She sat upright, not slumped over as she worked on her computer. Her auburn hair was thick and wavy and fell down her back. He imagined it would feel like silk when he wove his fingers in it. His cock hardened at the thought. *Fuck!* If he didn't get control of himself, this woman would have him coming in his pants, and it had been a couple decades since he had that happen. At that thought, he sauntered into her office, closing and locking the door behind him.

"Mr. Dorsey," Elizabeth exclaimed, after turning her head to the sound of the door closing and seeing him standing in her office.

"Are you married, Elizabeth?" he asked roughly.

"Excuse me?" She turned completely in her chair. Her suit jacket was unbuttoned and her pale green camisole clung tightly to her full breasts. His cock stiffened even more at the sight.

"I don't see a ring on your finger, but that doesn't mean anything these days. Are you married?" he asked again. He stood in front of her desk with his arms crossed over his chest.

"No," she said with a confused look on her face.

"Are you seeing anyone? Sleeping with anyone?" he asked further.

"What?" she said, standing up from her chair. Her face was incapable of hiding her shock at his questions. Her green eyes were wide. Her lips parted. "What sort of questions are these?" John's stride made short use of the distance between them. He stood directly in front of her, cornering her behind her desk. He looked down into her green eyes. They were gorgeous... she was gorgeous. And he had every intention of claiming her.

"Answer my questions, Elizabeth. Are you seeing anyone?" He watched as her eyes widened even further with shock at his determination to get answers to his questions. Nervousness flittered across her face, but her breath came out in short pants as if his close proximity affected her. He watched as her chest rose and fell with each breath. *God, he wanted to feel her body against his.* He just knew she would feel perfect against him... in his arms.

"Your questions are inappropriate," she replied sharply. Despite her body giving her attraction away, she held firm. He liked that. He liked a woman that wasn't too easy of a catch.

"I agree," he said, impatiently. "They are inappropriate. I need the answers nonetheless."

"Why?" she asked. Her gaze scanned his face as if looking for the answer to her question.

"Answer me," he demanded. His hand reached out and caressed her cheek as if to soothe the harshness of his words.

"You are way out of line, Mr. Dorsey," Elizabeth said.

"Yes, I know," he said a little softer this time. His fingers tucked a few strands of her hair behind her ear. His gaze dropped to her bared neck. He had to fight the urge to nuzzle the spot just below her ear. "But I need to know if there are any obstacles to making you mine. Are you seeing anyone?"

"No," she whispered. "I'm not seeing anyone." Her lips parted for a moment before she bit down on her lower lip. That was almost his undoing.

"Are you fucking anyone?" he asked. She released her bottom lip and sucked in a breath when he asked that question. Her gaze fell from his eyes to his lips and then to her hands. He placed his fingers under her chin and tilted her head up to meet his gaze again. He wanted to see her eyes when she answered him. There was heat in her gaze, and that thrilled him.

"No, Mr. Dorsey, I'm not *fucking* anyone at the moment," she said. Her voice was hard, but he heard the desire in it and that snapped his restraint. His hand weaved into her hair until his palm gripped the back of her head, pulling her into him. His mouth slammed down on hers. Her full lips were soft and pliable, and his tongue flicked out over her lips to taste her. She tasted so sweet…like candy. Her hands slid up his torso to his chest and he couldn't stop the growl that escaped him just from the feel of her hands on him.

"Mr. Dorsey," she breathed, pulling her head back and pushing on his chest to create some space between them. She looked up at him, trepidation in her eyes.

"No worries, Elizabeth," he said, running his thumb across her bottom lip.

"No worries?" she said, sharply. "You just kissed me!" Her hands were still placing pressure on his chest.

"I know," John said, with a little laugh. "And I'm going to do it again." He leaned down and pressed his lips gently against hers despite the force of her hands against his chest. With his hand in her hair, he pulled gently, tilting her head back just slightly, so he had a better angle for the kiss. He slipped his tongue against the seam of her lips and when she gasped, he used that opportunity to penetrate her mouth with his tongue. *Oh God!* She tasted like heaven. He knew the moment he saw her he would love the way she tasted…the way she felt. No woman had ever affected him like this. His tongue explored the cavern of her mouth, licking at the roof of it, at her teeth, tangling with her tongue. She moaned when he deepened the kiss even further, and their tongues danced sensually together.

Her hands slid up his chest and around his neck, pulling his whole body closer. He moved forward, backing her up against her desk. He pressed his pelvis into her. He had been right. Her body felt amazing against his. John's hands slid down her arms and over her hips until they settled at the small of her back. He pulled her further into him and groaned at the feel of her body pressing against his rock hard cock. Their kiss became almost manic. Her hands went into his hair and he practically dry-humped her against the desk. He was seconds from hiking her skirt up and burying himself between her thighs. The only thing that prevented that from happening was the interruption of her desk phone ringing.

"Oh shit," she said, pushing back on him again to regain her space. She reached for her desk phone.

"Elizabeth Wright. Can I help you?" Her breathing was ragged. Her face flushed. Her hands ran through her hair trying to straighten out her appearance. "Ok. Yes. I can make the meeting at 2. See you then." She placed the receiver back on the phone and turned to face him. "I'm sorry. We got carried away."

"Don't apologize, Elizabeth," John said, taking a step towards her. "I wanted to get carried away. The moment you walked into that board room this morning, I wanted nothing else but to get carried away with you. I have been unable to focus... unable to think straight."

"Mr. Dorsey, you sit on the board of directors of the company that employs me," she said, breathless. "Clearly, this is a conflict."

"Nothing in my director agreement even hints that I am not allowed to date an employee of the company," he said. "Nothing."

"Mr. Dorsey, it would be an ethical conflict. You assist in making decisions for the company as a whole. Any hint of impropriety—that a relationship with an employee influenced the way you voted—could ruin your term as a director and perhaps affect my career." Elizabeth straightened out her camisole and her jacket, buttoning the two buttons on the jacket. *Damn it!*

"Elizabeth, I'm not taking no for an answer," John said. "Whatever is between us will not affect my role as a member of the board, I promise you. So, I'll pick you up after work today. We'll do dinner. There is nothing that is going to stop 'this' from happening." He waved his hand between the two of them signifying what he meant by "this." He leaned in and placed a kiss on her cheek. "And please call me John," he whispered in her ear. He saw her shiver when his lips brushed the skin just below her ear.

At that, he turned and walked to the door, unlocking and opening it before walking through it. He knew if he looked back, she would be standing there staring at him, and he didn't want to give her the opportunity to turn down dinner. He headed back upstairs to the board to enjoy his lunch with a shit-eating grin on his face. *Christ, this board day couldn't move fast enough.*

Chapter Four

Elizabeth's two o'clock meeting bled into her three o'clock meeting, so she didn't make it back towards her office until almost four-thirty. She struggled to keep John and their kiss from her thoughts the entire afternoon, but it was a complete failure. She was in big trouble. This could ruin her in so many ways... he could ruin her. Even if John's board of directors' agreement didn't forbid a relationship between them, clearly it would be frowned upon. Maybe it could even affect her job. She loved her job. And her heart... she wasn't the type of girl that could keep her heart out of things for long. She didn't know if she could keep things strictly sexual. John didn't seem to be the type of guy that put his heart into things. He seemed more like that type that would fuck her brains out once or twice and call it a day. Could she handle that? Despite all the warnings shooting off in her head, she didn't think she'd have much resistance in her if he kissed her again like he had earlier. Her whole body reacted so strongly to him. She took a deep breath, and breezed into the legal department heading toward the hallway to her office.

"Liz," Roni said, grabbing her attention before she blew right by. Elizabeth stopped and turned to face Corbin's assistant. A smile stretched across Roni's lips.

"Yes, Roni," Elizabeth replied. She couldn't quite figure out the look of sheer happiness that was written all over Roni's face.

"Mr. Dorsey called down from executive about thirty minutes ago," she said with a smile. Now, Elizabeth understood. John Dorsey could get any woman to wear a ridiculously silly grin by simply saying his name. "He said his Town Car will pick you up at four-thirty downstairs."

"What?" Elizabeth sputtered. So much for being discreet. Though she loved Roni to death, she did tend to be a gossiper. Within the first week of working at Advantage, Roni had supplied Elizabeth with the dirt on everyone in the department and beyond.

"It's already four-thirty, Liz," Roni continued. "I suggest you hurry. You don't want to keep a man like that waiting on you too long." Roni winked at her. *Oh God!* Elizabeth turned on her heels and walked quickly down the short hallway to her office. She did a quick check of her email before turning off her computer, grabbing her purse and ducking out the back stairs to get down to the first floor. No reason to give Roni, or anyone else for that matter, more reason to gossip.

As she walked out the front door of their building in downtown St. Petersburg, a black Lincoln Town Car sat idling at the curb. A man in a pair of black slacks and a white shirt jumped out of the driver's seat and hurried around the car to open the door for her.

"Ms. Wright," he said, opening the back door. She wasn't used to this sort of thing. She grew up on the lower side of middle class where people drove their own cars around and no one waited on her, except her mother when she was ill.

As she ducked through the car door, she saw John sitting there. His white shirt was unbuttoned at the collar and his sleeves were rolled up his forearms. *Yep, he definitely worked out.* She could see the muscle definition just in his forearms. And his hands... even his hands looked strong. She remembered the feel of them on her low back when he pulled her against him earlier. Her cheeks flushed as the memory of their kiss invaded her mind. A flush spread all over her body. She could feel the heat pool at her core. She crouched onto the black leather seat and set her purse between them. Perhaps a little barrier would do them good.

"Mr. Dorsey," she said softly as the driver closed the door behind her.

"Elizabeth, please call me John. When I'm buried deep inside your body, I don't want you moaning 'Mr. Dorsey,' I want you calling me by my first name," he said. His hazel eyes turned a shade darker as he spoke his words, but his gaze never left her eyes. She inhaled sharply. Quickly scanning the car, she let out her breath when she realized the barrier between the front and the back of the vehicle was up, making their conversation private. *Thank God!* She'd never been around anyone who had been so frank about wanting to fuck her. Should she be pissed? He clearly assumed bedding her was a foregone conclusion.

"That's quite presumptuous of you, John," she said, drawing out his name. She could do this. She wasn't a woman without any game or flirting abilities. He growled when she said his name and crossed the distance between them, pushing her purse to the car floor and pinning her against the back seat. His hand gripped the back of her head just seconds before his lips pressed against hers. This man knew how to kiss. His lips were soft but strong and confident against her own. He worked her lips open and slipped his tongue inside, exploring her. The feel of his tongue against hers made her moan.

"I love the way you just said my name," he whispered against her mouth. "I can't wait to hear you say it when I first slide inside your hot little body." Elizabeth whimpered at his words. Something about him made her feel sexier than she ever had. She just wanted to feel him above her and at this moment, she didn't care where they were.

Her hands wrapped around his neck and pulled him even more into her. She took a little initiative with their kiss. She pushed her tongue into his mouth, so that it danced sensually with his tongue. One hand slid down his shoulder and over his sculpted bicep. Every aspect of his body was hard. She could feel his muscles twitch underneath her hand. She sucked on his tongue and he growled. Her tongue laved against his and explored his mouth further.

John's hand slid down the side of her body until it made contact with her knee. His hand was warm and callused against her skin, causing her entire body to feel like it was on fire. Slowly, he inched his hand up the inside of her leg and under her skirt until his fingers danced lightly over her lace panties, which were already damp with her juices. His fingers worked her clit through the lace until she was panting against his mouth. She could feel the first hints of her orgasm approaching. She was going to come, fully dressed, in the back of his car! *Fuck! He owned her.* Pushing her panties aside, his fingers moved over her slick folds. Elizabeth cried out at the feel of his fingers against the most sensitive part of her. It almost pushed her over the edge.

"Not yet," he whispered. Pushing his tongue into her mouth, he penetrated her pussy with his finger. Elizabeth gasped at the invasion to her body. Since walking into the board room earlier today, she had envisioned numerous times what his hands would feel like on her body, but this was more than she imagined. Her body yearned for him. Her back arched off the seat and her pelvis writhed against the heel of his hand. "That's it, sweetheart. Come for me." He plunged a second finger in her pussy and curled them both until they touched a part inside of her she didn't even know existed. He stroked her there until her entire body came off the seat and her orgasm rocked her. Her pussy quivered and spasmed around his fingers, pulling them further into her body. Her vision blurred before all she could see was stars. This wasn't her first orgasm, by any stretch of the imagination, but it was most definitely the first orgasm like that.

"Oh my God," she breathed as her body finally slumped against the seat. His fingers were still buried inside her body, stroking her through the last few spasms. Her breath was ragged. John brought his mouth down on hers, kissing her gently, nuzzling her bottom lip between his teeth.

"That... that was fucking amazing to watch," he said, pulling back from their kiss and staring into her eyes. He slipped his fingers from her body and brought them to his mouth. Sliding both fingers between his lips, she watched as he tasted her juices on his fingers. She couldn't stifle the groan that ripped through her. She'd never seen anything quite so erotic. "Fuck, you taste good. You have no idea how bad I want to take you right now. Right here. But we should only be a few minutes from our destination. And if I don't stop now, I will be fucking you for the first time against the back seat of this car and you deserve better than that." Elizabeth didn't know what made her more faint: watching him taste her off his own fingers, or his words "first time" as if there would be more than one time...or that he felt she deserved better than a quick fuck in the car.

"Don't get me wrong," he whispered hoarsely, interrupting her thoughts. "I will fuck you on the back seat of this car. Most likely, more than once. I just don't want it to be our first time." She straightened up in the seat, still lightheaded from the mind-blowing orgasm and his titillating words. She pushed her fingers through her long, now tangled, mane. She couldn't imagine what she looked like right then. Quite honestly, she didn't care.

Chapter Five

Looking out the car window, Elizabeth watched as John's car pulled into a driveway. She had been so wrapped up in John that she hadn't even noticed that they were heading towards the beach. Her eyes widened like saucers. The Spanish-style house was three stories and sat right on the beach. The exterior was a dark yellow with a reddish-orange tiled roof. Multiple floor-to-ceiling windows peppered the top two floors.

"Where are we?" she asked. Her gaze continued to scan the house.

"My home," he said, opening his car door and holding his hand out for her. She could hear the sound of waves crashing to shore in the distance. Slowly, she scooted across the seat, grabbing her purse from the floor and taking his hand. Standing on the driveway, she straightened her skirt before her head fell back to take in his beautiful home.

"You live here?" she breathed the question.

"Yes," he chuckled. "When I'm not traveling for work." His hand still had a hold on hers and he entwined their fingers as he started walking towards the large wooden front door. He knocked on the driver's side window when they passed, and the car started to pull away.

"It's beautiful." Growing up, both her parents worked their asses off as school teachers just to make the payments on their small ranch-styled house and cars. She had to take out school loans for college and law school. Even with all the money she made the first several years with Barnes and Simon, she never imagined she'd ever be able to afford a house like this.

"It's just a house," John said lightly. He unlocked the front door and held it open so she could walk through.

"This is more than just a house," Elizabeth said, looking around at her surroundings. The foyer was small with dark hardwood floors and cream colored walls. A teal-painted console table stood flush against the right wall. It looked worn… exactly like something one would find in a coastal home. A round mirror hung over the table and a vase of fresh Gerber daisies in bright pink and orange sat in the center of the table. "Did you build this house?" she asked, looking at him. Though she knew little about him, she did know he ran his own construction company.

"Yes, I did," he said proudly. "I had my architect friend design it and then I built it… with some help from my contractor friends, of course." He smiled at her and she felt her knees weaken just a bit. He had a smile that could turn her into a puddle of lust and desire in an instant. The air was charged between them. She could feel the electricity all but crackle against her skin. She had never experienced anything like John Dorsey.

Elizabeth noticed the hardwood stairs to the left that clearly led to the second level, but John pulled her towards a white door straight in front of them. He opened the door and Elizabeth's mouth fell open.

"Your house has an elevator?" she asked. Her eyes once again were saucers.

"Yes," he laughed. "I rarely use it. I usually take the stairs, but I'm taking you straight to the third floor." He pulled her into the elevator and closed the door and the gate before pressing the button to go up. Just as the elevator started to move upwards, John pinned her against the wall. She dropped her purse on the elevator floor. His thumb caressed her cheek, then her bottom lip before lifting her chin so he could look into her eyes.

"I know I promised you dinner, and I will keep that promise. But I need to be inside you, Elizabeth. I don't know why I feel this so desperately, but I do. I need to feel that tight little pussy wrapped around my cock. I need to feel you come all over me." He pressed his pelvis against her as his lips came down hard on her mouth. Elizabeth whimpered at his words and at the feel of his hard cock pressed against her abdomen. God, she wanted fuck him. His tongue flicked across the seam of her lips, which parted easily to allow him access to her mouth. Pushing into her mouth, his tongue danced with hers. His hand weaved into her hair and pulled her head to the side, so his lips could kiss their way down the side of her neck, nipping at her flesh. Her head fell back against the elevator wall as her hands slid down the front of his chest and started unbuttoning his white shirt. Once unbuttoned, she slid her hands up his chiseled abdomen and over his smooth chest. A groan tore from his lips.

"Don't take your hands off me," he growled. His lips came back to hers. He sucked her bottom lip into his mouth before biting down on it. His tongue flicked where he bit to soothe the sting. Then, he bit her again. Elizabeth couldn't control the sounds escaping her. His hands began to work feverishly on her clothes. He undid the buttons of her of her suit jacket and ripped it down her arms, tossing it on the floor of the small elevator. He pulled her pale green camisole out of her skirt and up over her head. He reached behind her and unzipped her skirt, pushing it down over her hips until it pooled at her feet. She stood before him in nothing but her nude lace bra, matching lace panties and her taupe heels. His hands slid up her hips and over her bra, cupping her breasts. His thumbs grazed over her already hard nipples.

"Christ, Elizabeth, you are even more beautiful than I imagined," he said, leaning back and admiring her body. His hand slid around to her back and with his nimble fingers, he unhooked her bra with ease. Clearly, he had some experience with a bra. It fell forward and he brushed it down her arms, allowing her full breasts to fall into his waiting hands. He cupped her naked breasts, kneading them. He leaned forward and took a nipple into his mouth. His tongue flicked over her nipple and Elizabeth moaned loudly. He kissed and nipped her breast before sucking her other nipple into his mouth. John's hand molded and caressed her other breast.

"John," she sighed. He pulled his head away from her breast and looked at her. The back of his hand caressed her cheek. "I need you inside me." She pushed her hands over his shoulders and down his arms until he was shirtless. Then her hands worked eagerly on the button and zipper of his slacks.

"Fuck," he growled. "Say it again."

"I need you inside me," she whispered. She had never been so turned on in her life. Her body ached for him. He pushed the gate aside and opened the door of the elevator into a room that took Elizabeth's breath away. The entire end of the room was walled with floor-to-ceiling windows that overlooked the Gulf of Mexico. It was a breath-taking view and the sun was just beginning to set. The sky was a beautiful rainbow of yellow, orange and pink streaks.

John pulled her from the elevator towards his large king-sized bed, leaving the door open and most of their clothes on the floor of the elevator. His pants barely clung to his hips. Elizabeth watched as he pushed them down his legs along with his black boxer briefs. *Good God, he was huge!* She had known he would be big from the feel of him against her earlier, but to see him standing there, his cock jutting out, fully erect, left her in awe. He was fucking gorgeous. He prowled towards her and pushed her back on his bed. His hand reached for his nightstand and he pulled out a condom.

"Elizabeth, this isn't going to be slow or soft. I'm going to fuck you hard. I need to fuck you hard," he said as he tore the condom from its wrapper and rolled it over his engorged cock. Once the condom was on, his hand slid under the side of her lace panties and tore them from her body. She gasped as she watched him toss what was left of her panties on the floor. "I've been hard since the moment you walked into that board room this morning and have wanted nothing other than to be buried inside you." His fingers slipped through her folds, making sure she was wet enough for him. Elizabeth mewled at the feel of his fingers on her pussy again. It was a feeling she was sure she would never tire of.

"I don't want you to go slow or soft, John," she whispered. Her hand slid down the front of his body and gripped his cock, squeezing him.

"Uh-uh," he said, seizing her hand. "I'm so fucking on the edge right now that feeling your sweet little hand around me will make me explode." He crawled onto the bed and between her legs, pushing her legs further apart so she could accommodate his hips. "I'm not going to last long as it is. But I promise, I will thoroughly explore every inch of your beautiful body later." With that, he pulled his hips back and entered her to the hilt. A feral cry escaped him and Elizabeth's breath caught in her chest. He was huge and it took her body some time to adjust to his length and girth. "Holy shit, you are so fucking tight. Fuck!" He held himself still on his forearms, with his cock buried all the way inside her. She felt him at the very end of her. Sweat beaded across his forehead. She could tell he was trying to hold back, but his restraint was waning. His hazel eyes gazed down at her with concern, as if to check to make sure she was okay... that he hadn't hurt her. Her hand wrapped around the nape of his neck and pulled him down to her. Her tongue flicked out and over his lips.

"Fuck me, John," she said. He groaned as his mouth came down hard on hers and his hips began relentlessly pounding against her body. He pinned her to the bed with his thrusts. Their groans and moans blended together as he pumped in and out of her. Elizabeth could feel the wave of ecstasy wash over her. With each thrust of his hips, her clit ground into his pelvis, sending shockwaves through her body. "Oh God," she yelled. "Oh God!" She couldn't hold back another second. Her body came completely undone underneath him, and she splintered into a million pieces as her pussy gripped his cock even tighter.

"Fuck," he grunted. "That's it, sweetheart. Come all over my cock." He continued to pound into her until his body stiffened and his cock pulsed inside her. His breath was labored and he held himself perfectly still for several seconds before he collapsed on top of her. She could feel his heart pounding against her own.

"Are you okay?" she asked with a little giggle. She wasn't a virgin. She'd had her share of sexual experiences throughout her life, but nothing compared to this.

"I don't know," John said, raising his head and looking down at her. "That was fucking unbelievable. Your tight little body was made for me, sweetheart." He leaned down and kissed the tip of her nose softly before pulling out of her body and sliding next to her. His arm wrapped around her and pulled her to him. "I can't wait to do that again…and again," he said with a smile.

Chapter Six

John walked out of his en suite bathroom after cleaning up and throwing on a pair jeans. He stopped in his tracks at the sight before him. Elizabeth stood at the wall of windows, wearing nothing but his white button down shirt. She was staring out at the Gulf of Mexico. The sun had set and the twilight cast beautiful colors around her. Her auburn hair glistened, falling down her back. He could see the muscle tone in her hamstrings and calves below the hem of his shirt. She had the kind of body that made him want to drop to his knees and worship her.

He quietly walked up behind her and slid his arms around her waist. She sighed and leaned her head back against his chest.

"You look beautiful standing here like this," he said, kissing the top of her head.

"This view is breathtaking. I hope you don't mind that I threw your shirt on. I didn't want to put my stuffy suit back on and I didn't want to rifle through your drawers." She tilted her head up to look at him.

"I don't mind at all," he replied. He bent his head down and placed a gentle kiss on her lips. "Are you hungry?"

"Famished," she said.

"Good. Dinner is downstairs in the oven. I spend a few hours on weekends cooking meals. I asked Lori, my housekeeper, to pull the veal scaloppini from the freezer and put it in the oven before she left today. It should be ready by now." He took her hand and pulled her towards the staircase that led down to the main part of the house.

"Veal scaloppini?" she asked. "You know how to cook that?"

"Of course. My mother is Italian. She taught me how to cook just about anything. I enjoy doing it." The look of surprise on Elizabeth's face made him chuckle. "Why do you seem so surprised?"

"I just don't know many men that know how to cook, let alone enjoy it," she said with a shy smile. *God, she was adorable!* They entered his fully decked-out Tuscan-style kitchen. "Wow! No wonder you like to cook. This kitchen is amazing!"

"Thanks," John said. "I designed it myself. My mom likes to come over and cook with me sometimes, so I wanted something we could both enjoy." Elizabeth's face softened at the mention of him spending time with his mom. He leaned in and kissed her softly on the forehead before grabbing an oven mitt from a drawer and pulling the glass casserole dish out of the oven. He set the dish on the counter and grabbed two plates from a cupboard. The smell of veal scaloppini wafted through the kitchen.

"Mmmm," she moaned. "Smells delicious."

"I assure you, it is not as delicious as you, Elizabeth, but it will be good," he said, winking at her. John loved to see her flush every time he complimented her. Color looked good on her. "Would you like a glass of white wine?"

"That would be lovely," Elizabeth replied. "Can I help with anything?"

"No," he said, walking over to the wine fridge and pulling out a bottle of Sauvignon blanc. "Sit, please. This is my house. And you are my guest." He pointed to the small glass table in the breakfast nook. He watched as she slid onto a cushioned chair and sat cross-legged. He could definitely get used to having her around.

He plated their food and poured two glasses of wine. Placing her plate and wine in front of her, he pulled the other chair next to her and sat down with his own food. Eagerly, they began to eat their meals.

"God, this is amazing," she said, biting into a piece of veal. Her tongue swept out and over her lips. John felt his cock stiffen. She took another bite and did the same thing with her tongue. *She was so fucking sexy and didn't even know it!*

"I'm glad you like it," he said, hoarsely. He couldn't disguise the arousal that crept into his voice. He took another couple bites of his food, but his eyes never left her. He watched as she ate most of her plate of food. He loved it. He loved a woman not afraid to eat.

"You're an amazing cook, John," she said, softly. She took another bite of her food and moaned. It was the moan that did him in.

He dropped his fork on his plate before leaning over and pressing his lips to hers. She tasted good enough to eat. Working his lips over hers, his tongue slipped out and between the seam of her lips. When her lips parted, he glided his tongue into her mouth, tasting her. His tongue explored every part of her mouth. He wanted to devour her.

"John," she moaned, setting her fork on her plate. His hands pulled her legs from their criss-crossed position and he slid to his knees on the floor in front of her, never breaking their kiss. Slowly, he unbuttoned his shirt that she was wearing and exposed her luscious body to him. His hands cupped her full breasts and he rolled her already hard nipples between his thumb and forefinger. He was sure he could spend forever exploring her body and never get tired of it.

Breaking their kiss, he reached for her glass of wine. Slowly, he poured some wine down her chest and over her breasts. She inhaled sharply as the chilled wine hit her skin. Her nipples pebbled even more. Setting the wine glass back on the table, John leaned forward and ran his tongue up from her belly button to between her breasts. Then he did it again. His tongue laved up her body, stopping to suckle her nipples along the way. Her back arched into him and her hips moved to the edge of the chair, seeking contact with his body.

"This vintage has never tasted better," he breathed against her body, lapping up every last drop of wine on her torso. Pushing her against the back of the chair, he grabbed the wine glass again and poured a little over the short, soft hairs covering her pussy. He set the glass back on the table. Leaning forward, his tongue lapped up her slick folds. "I take that back," he said between swipes at her clit with his tongue. "This vintage has never tasted better than it does right now." His thumbs separated her lips and he eagerly buried his tongue inside her. Her hips lifted off the chair and her hand gripped his hair, pulling his face even further into her. The wine combined with her juices was an aphrodisiac he could get used to.

"Fuck," she cried out. His tongue laved up her slit before circling her clit. His looked up her. Her head hung back. Her eyes were closed tight. Closing his lips over her clit, he sucked on it. Her eyes shot open and their gazes met. His cock was straining against his jeans. Watching her come apart before him was amazing. Her thighs started to quiver around him. He slid a hand up her leg and penetrated her with two fingers, stroking that area inside her he knew would take her over the edge. "Oh, God!" Her pussy squeezed his fingers tightly before her whole body shook as she rode out her orgasm. He removed his fingers from inside her and lapped up all the juices that flowed from her sex.

"I want to fuck you," Elizabeth said, pushing his head back and sliding onto his lap, straddling him. Her fingers made short work of the button and zipper of his jeans. Hearing her words and feeling her hand reach inside of his jeans and wrap around his cock made him moan. The jeans had been their only barrier. She opened the fly of his jeans as wide as possible in the position he was in and pulled him free. Rising up on her knees , she impaled herself on his cock.

"Holy fuck," he yelled. The skin-to-skin contact… the slickness of her vaginal walls clamping down on his cock was more than he could handle. He had never had sex with a woman without a condom. He was always so very careful. Even with his ex, he used a condom. His friends always told him he was missing out. He had no idea. *Jesus Christ!* The feeling was unbelievable. She rocked in his lap, throwing her head back and moaning. He grabbed her hips and held her still. "Elizabeth, I don't have a condom on," he said. His words came out raspy because the feel of her tight, wet pussy covering him completely made it hard for him to breathe.

"John," she whispered, leaning forward next to his ear. "I'm clean. I promise you. I trust that you are too. And I'm on the pill." She nibbled his ear lobe between her teeth before pulling back and staring into his eyes. "Can I fuck you now?" The growl that tore through his chest surprised even him. Any hesitation he had was quickly absolved with her words and the feel of her gripping him.

"Fuck, yes," he replied. He released his tight grip on her hips. She immediately started gliding up and down his cock. Pressing her lips against his mouth, she circled her hips, grounding her clit into his pelvis. Dipping his tongue into her mouth, he swallowed her moan. His hands roamed over her smooth body, touching every part of her, as she worked him over. He'd never felt anything this intimate. He'd never had a woman take so much control over his pleasure and her own. John knew he was only minutes away from erupting inside of her, but he wanted her to come again. He slid his hand down the front of her body over her abdomen until he found her mound. His thumb circled her clit before putting light pressure on the hard bundle of nerves.

"Fuck," Elizabeth screamed, tearing her mouth from his. Her hands gripped his shoulders tight, digging her nails into his skin. She threw her head back as he began to pump his hips up to meet hers. She exploded. Her pussy had a vise grip on his cock. He'd never felt anything like it.

"Oh fuck, sweetheart, I'm going to come," John cried out as he felt the spasm of her pussy pull him further over the edge. "Fuck!" His hips bucked wildly as he ground out his orgasm in her hot tightness. "Fuck!" His arms wrapped around her as she collapsed on top of him. They were both breathing hard. He held her for several minutes and her arms tightened around his neck. *He wanted this woman!*

"A girl could get used to this, you know," Elizabeth said, picking her head up off his shoulder and looking at him. Her green eyes sparkled. Her skin glistened with sweat. Her legs still straddled his. "Amazing home-cooked meals. Fabulous wine. Breathtaking views. Multiple orgasms. I can't believe you're still single." He chuckled.

"I'm single by choice," he said, placing a gentle kiss on her nose. "But I'm thinking I want to change that status. I've got it bad for you, Elizabeth. Very bad."

"Bad enough to let me stay the night?" she asked with a smile and a wink.

"It's worse than that, sweetheart! Let's start with you staying here the weekend and go from there! A guy could get used to having you around… permanently," he said, placing a rough kiss on her lips.

"Permanently?" Elizabeth asked, pulling back from the kiss. He looked in her green eyes and saw nothing but joy. She appeared as happy as he was. He nodded his head. Her hands cupped his face on either side and she placed a soft kiss on his lips.

"You can't possibly think I'm going to let you go," he said with a smile. John ran his hands up her back and pulled her into his embrace. For the first time in a long time, he felt extremely happy and at peace. "Now that I have you, I'm going to keep you."

"I'd like that," Elizabeth said, leaning into him and snuggling into his chest. "I'd like that a lot."

The End

TAKING ADVANTAGE

DEDICATION

To my husband, who allows me to escape into my "writing cave" enough to live my dream! Thank you!

To Natalie - For beta reading this story and giving me your honest feedback! Thank you so much, girlfriend!

TAKING ADVANTAGE

BOARD APPROVED

Taking Advantage, 2

Jessica Jayne

Copyright © 2013

Chapter One

"Flipping fudge," Gregory Snow heard a soft female voice say from behind him. He could tell the delicate voice was upset, but he couldn't help but chuckle. After years practicing law, it was strange to hear someone swear so kindly. In fact, he was pretty sure the last time he heard someone say "fudge" to replace the f-word, he had been watching television on Thanksgiving and A Christmas Story was on. He spun around to find the friendly curser and didn't see anyone.

"Freaking flip," he heard her again. Then he saw the lithe body of a woman rise from behind an older purple VW bug he had just passed in the parking lot and he lost his ability to breathe. Holy Christ! Her curly golden hair was pulled back in a tight ponytail, wispy curls framing her face. She wore a thin purple and hot pink braided headband in an effort to tame her blonde mane. Her hot pink tank top clung tightly to her torso, showing off her small but perky breasts. Greg's cock hardened as his gaze scanned over what he could see of her. She was stunning. She looked like she was coming from a workout, which puzzled him since she was in the parking lot of Advantage Insurance Company.

"Can I help you?" he asked. The woman startled at the sound of his voice. When she lifted her eyes to meet his, Greg inhaled sharply. She had the deepest blue eyes he'd ever seen. They were gorgeous. She was gorgeous. She couldn't be more than twenty-five… maybe twenty-six. There was not a single line on her face. Everything on her that was visible to him was tight. He imagined her pussy would also be tight. What? Where the hell did that come from? She screamed youth… much too young for him, at forty-two, to be thinking such thoughts. But he couldn't stop the arousal that immediately coursed through him at the sight of her. Something about her turned him inside out.

"I'm…I'm sorry," she said, standing a little taller. She might be five feet four inches… maybe. She threw what looked like a rolled-up yoga mat over her shoulder, walked around the back of the VW and lifted the hatch to throw her mat inside. "My car seems to have died and I don't have the slightest idea what's wrong with it. And I have a class to teach in exactly thirty-five minutes and it takes me about thirty minutes to get to the studio without traffic. Triple A will take at least forty-five minutes to get here. By that time, I've missed my class at the studio. It's too late to call for a substitute to teach the class. The studio is so new. I can't afford to lose any customers at this point." She took a deep breath and Greg watched as her chest rose and fell with her breath. His gaze lowered to her tight black yoga capri pants. Damn! She had a rocking body. Lean, muscular legs. Perky ass. What was going on with him? Had it really been that long since he'd been laid that he was lusting after this young stranger? She was going to think he was an old creep. "Shizzle!" His gaze flew from her ass to her face again at her exclamation.

"Did you just say 'shizzle'?" he asked. It was impossible to hide the humor in his voice. This beautiful creature was unreal. She looked like a Victoria's Secret angel with her long blonde hair and tight body, yet she swore like a kindergartner.

She slammed the hatch down and kicked her rear bumper. When she looked up at him, he could see the tears welling up in her eyes, so he quickly wiped his hand over his face to keep the smile from spreading further across his lips.

"I'm sorry," he said softly. He hated to see women cry, especially ones that made him hornier than a teenager. "Can I drive you to the studio? You can deal with your car later. I can tell it's important to you."

"Seriously? You'd do that?" she asked, tilting her head up to look at him.

"Of course," Greg said softly. Before he could even take his next breath, this blonde beauty threw herself at him.

"Thank you," she said into his chest. Slowly, his arms wrapped around her small tight body and he gave her a gentle squeeze. Then he grabbed her by the shoulders and pushed her back, fearing if she stayed that close to him, she'd surely feel his straining erection and that would probably make her less thankful for his assistance.

"It's not a problem." He pulled his keys out of his pocket and hit the unlock button to his black BMW SUV. The lights flashed and he watched as her gaze fell on his vehicle. "I'm Greg, by the way. Greg Snow." He held out his hand. Her head slowly turned back toward him. After just throwing herself at him seconds ago, he found it adorable that her cheeks were flushed when she slid her delicate hand into his. Her skin was so soft and yet an electric current shot through him at the feel of her hand in his.

"I'm Tessa Mills," she said softly. Her gaze fell to their joined hands before she raised her eyes to look him in the face. He wondered if she felt it, too. Then he saw it in her eyes. There was something in her deep blue eyes... heat... desire, maybe? He couldn't make it out exactly, but it was not a look he expected from her, considering their obvious age difference. But he liked it. A lot.

"Grab the things you need and jump in. I just need to make two calls before we head out, okay?" He watched as she reopened the hatch to her car and pulled out her mat and a purse. Pulling out his iPhone from his pants pocket, he quickly dialed his car mechanic.

"Jarod's," Greg heard his friend on the line.

"Hey, buddy. It's Greg. I need you to do me a favor," he said, watching Tessa walk the four cars down the aisle to his BMW. He could not get over her body. Youth definitely had its advantages. Not that the women he had been with in the more recent months didn't have good bodies, but they didn't have the kind of body Tessa had. What he wouldn't give to feel her wrapped around him in every way.

"Sure thing," Jarod said, bringing him out of his lusty haze. "Whatcha need?"

"Can you send your tow truck over to Advantage's parking lot to pick up a car?" Greg asked, his eyes still glued on Tessa.

"What's wrong with the Bimmer?"

"It's not my car," Greg said. He explained the situation to Jarod, who agreed to tow the VW Bug to his shop and take a look at it. "I'll drop the keys off shortly.

Just call me and let me know what's wrong with it. I'll cover the repairs." As he disconnected his call with Jarod, his phone began to buzz with another call. He noticed John Dorsey's number on his phone. "Dorsey," Greg said into his phone.

"Where the hell are you?"

"In the parking lot," Greg said, still watching Tessa. Just before she slid into the passenger seat of his BMW, she looked over her shoulder in Greg's direction and gave him the sexiest smile he had ever seen. He couldn't stifle the groan that escaped him.

"Did you just moan in my ear?" John asked with a chuckle.

"I think I did," Greg said with a laugh. "I'll tell you about it later. I'm going to be a bit late to this afternoon's session. I have to run someone across town quickly. I'll be back in less than an hour."

"Run who across town?" John asked with amusement. "Does she have anything to do with that moan?"

"Ha-ha, Dorsey! I'll bring you up to speed when I get back."

"What would you like me to tell Phillip and the board?" John asked. Out of all the board members, John was his favorite. He may have been one of the richest men in the area, owning the largest construction company around, Dorsey Construction, but he was the most levelheaded guy Greg knew. They really hit it off together. Greg considered John a friend. And since John had found Elizabeth Wright, the woman to settle him down, so-to-speak, he'd been trying to find Greg a companion, too. Any inclination that Greg was showing interest in a woman resulted in John's utmost attention.

"Tell them my errand took a little longer than anticipated," Greg said. "I promise to get there as soon as I can." He ended the call and made sure Tessa's car was locked before walking to his BMW. He slid into the driver seat and immediately started his car. He glanced over at Tessa and found her staring at him with those big blue eyes. And those eyes were not showing any concern over their age difference. They were scanning over every inch of him like she might be considering him for dinner. The look on her face caused his cock to stiffen again. Shit! This was going to be a long drive!

Chapter Two

Tessa stared at the man that slid into the driver's seat and a sudden wave of lust swept through her. He was one hundred percent male and she was totally enthralled. He was incredibly handsome. Older than her... maybe thirty-five. She had never been really good at guessing ages, but she did know he was older than her twenty-seven years. His navy dress slacks had done nothing to hide his strong muscular thighs, and the white button down shirt made it obvious that Greg was not your average male build. He was built strong. She had felt it when she threw herself at him for his generous offer to drive her to her studio. Was she crazy? She threw herself into a complete stranger's arms! And then she got into his car! Her mother would have her committed immediately if she found out. Shoot! Her alcoholic mother would try to have her committed for anything if it meant she had access to Tessa's bank account and Tessa was "out of her hair."

For some reason, Greg didn't scare her at all. Perhaps it was his soft grey eyes that assured her he posed no danger to her. All she knew was what her gut told her: she wouldn't end up in a ditch on the side of the road. Her body hummed, telling her this man could take her places she'd never been.

"Where are we headed?" Greg asked, putting the BMW in reverse and pulling out of the parking space. He maneuvered the car with ease. Tessa was impressed with how smooth and graceful his movements were, considering his size.

"Yoga You," Tessa replied. "It's my yoga studio on Treasure Island. Take First Avenue North all the way to the end. Then make a left on 66th Street and a right on

Central. I can direct you once we reach the island." She sat back against the tan leather seat and let out the breath she didn't realize she was holding. That stupid VW bug had been giving her problems lately. She bought it from a used car lot when she turned sixteen and had been driving it ever since. It was a great car, but she'd beat the hell out of it. She didn't always have the money to fix things right away, which led to problems getting bigger. This was the third time it had broken down in less than three months. But with the new studio open, she couldn't afford a new VW yet.

"I know how to get to Treasure Island," Greg said softly before winking at her. The wink sent a chill down her spine. Was he flirting with her? She could only hope. It was clear there was an age gap between them, but she didn't want him to look at her as some young girl. She wanted him to look at her as a woman because he set something afire inside of her that none of the guys her age could even spark. "I live there."

"You live there?" she asked with a hint of envy.

"Yes. I own a condo there. I figure if I'm going to live in Florida, I might as well live on the beach." He glanced over at her before pulling into traffic. He was sizing her up, checking out her reaction to his statements. He drove a top-of-the-line vehicle. He owned a condo on the beach. He dressed well. Obviously, he had money.

"Impressive," Tessa said and she meant it. "I've always dreamed of living on the beach. But I don't think my chosen career path is lucrative enough to own a house out there. I live in the Tyrone area." Greg nodded in recognition of the area.

"Being an entrepreneur is an amazing accomplishment," he said, weaving between traffic on First Avenue North through downtown St. Petersburg. "Now, I'm impressed."

"Thanks," Tessa replied, feeling the blush spread over her cheeks. What was it about this man that caused her body temperature to raise twenty degrees? "So, do you work at Advantage?"

"No. I'm a partner at Lowes & Kravitz here in St. Pete. I practice corporate law. But I'm a member of the board of directors at Advantage. That's why I was there," he said matter-of-factly. "It's board day."

"Oh flip," Tessa said softly. "I'm so sorry. I didn't realize I was keeping you away from something important. I'm sorry. You can drop me off at the next bus stop and I'll catch a ride to the studio."

"It's not a problem," Greg said with a smile. The car was stopped at a red light and he glanced over at her. "I promise you I don't mind at all." The heat in his gaze made the butterflies flutter in her belly.

"I imagine being on a board of directors is a pretty big deal and they expect you to be present. I feel horrible." She looked down at her hands resting in her lap. Here was this gorgeous man sitting next to her and she was in damsel-in-distress mode. She hated feeling helpless because she was anything but. She spent most of her life taking care of her mother, so Tessa didn't feel comfortable being in the role where someone was taking care of her. He must think she was incapable of taking care of herself and the things in her life. Another reason for him to think of her as a little girl and not an independent and sexy woman.

"Stop apologizing, Tessa," Greg said. "Everything will be fine. I'll head right back once I drop you off. What were you doing there?" He turned to look at her. His eyes were warm. He was interested. He wasn't just trying to make idle chit chat.

"I teach yoga in the gym on the first floor," she replied. "Advantage's HR was looking to do some classes for the employees on their lunch break. One of my friends works there in claims and she recommended me for yoga. I teach twice a week from noon to one." Her gaze swung up to look at him. His dark brown hair was very short on his head and sprinkled with a few greys just like his goatee. He was distinguished and he carried himself that way. It didn't surprise her that he was an attorney. He spoke eloquently and with such confidence. Clearly, he was way out of her league, and she wasn't sure why this revelation was such a huge disappointment to her being that they had only just met.

"That's great," he said, driving through the intersection once the light turned green. "So you own your own studio and teach at Advantage. I'd say you're pretty busy." She watched as he maneuvered through traffic and made a left on 66th St, headed for Central Avenue and then the bridge that would take them to Treasure Island.

"I am. I do two classes a day at the studio Monday through Saturday. I also do two classes a week at the county building for employees and then at Advantage," she explained. "And that's not to mention all the time I spend promoting and trying to drum up business. I'd like to be able to eventually hire another girl to help with the classes, so I don't have to be stretched so thin. But I'm not complaining... I swear. I love what I do." Shut up! When she was nervous, Tessa just didn't know how to stop talking and the verbal diarrhea just kept spilling from her lips.

"I don't want to seem like I am ungrateful for what I have. I've worked hard for it. Very hard. And..." Before she knew what was happening, Greg's hand palmed the back of her head and pulled her into a kiss that sent her head spinning. His lips were firm yet soft to the touch and he moved them expertly over her own. His goatee tickled her skin in a lascivious way that made her wonder what it would feel like at other spots on her body. His tongue flicked out over her lips and Tessa was unable to stifle the moan that rose up her chest. He took that as the opportunity to move further and pushed his tongue between her lips. Oh sweet Jesus, he tasted fantastic! He tasted like caramel coffee. She could get lost in his taste… in his kiss. His experience was evident as he licked into her mouth, exploring every crevice. His hand flexed at the back of her head before sliding down to the nape of her neck and caressing her there. She'd never been kissed so thoroughly, so sensuously. Her panties dampened as he took the kiss deeper and her hands gripped his shirt tightly as if it were the only way for her to keep from melting into the seat.

Beep! Beep! Startled back to reality by the cars honking behind them, Tessa pushed back from the kiss. She had been so wrapped up in her verbal dribble that she hadn't even recognized that they had been stopped at the light just before the bridge. And then his kiss threw her into a tailspin. She'd completely lost track of where she was. She came to, to find she was making out at a traffic light with a man she barely knew, and she was struggling to catch her breath after the make-out session.

"You'd better go," she whispered. She could feel the blush once again spread over her face. He looked at her closely, studying her. Another horn honked and his hand fell from the back of her neck and rested on her knee. He gave her a little squeeze and she watched as his lips quirked up into a gorgeous smile.

"I've been wanting to do that since the moment I laid eyes on you," he said, roughly. "And truth be told, I can't wait to do it again." Tessa inhaled sharply at his words and the desire behind them. He glanced over at her and smiled. His grey eyes were darker than they had been earlier, and she wondered if this was the look she'd read about countless times in all the romance novels she adored. "Where to, Tessa?" he asked. His question brought her back to the present.

"Uh… oh. Yeah. The Publix shopping plaza. I'm tucked away in there," she managed to stutter. It was obvious he was attracted to her. She could tell that by the look in his eyes and the way he kissed her. And if truths were being told, she was attracted to him too. Very much so. He was the sexiest thing she had ever seen. She could just tell from that kiss that he knew what he was doing. She was tired of the immaturity of the boys her age. They wanted to get laid and get drunk… and not in any particular order. And they weren't very good at either. Any orgasms she may have experienced over her limited sexual history were sadly all self-induced.

She hadn't been on a date in four months since her heart was broken by Tom, who after two weeks of dating and finally giving in to his demands sexually, informed her that he was married. But was jumping into the sack with someone she didn't know really the answer to her romantic woes? What if Greg was married? She didn't see a ring on his finger, but that didn't mean anything. Tom hadn't had a ring either. What if all Greg wanted was a quick roll between the sheets? Could her heart handle that again? Her heart? Really? She just met Greg minutes before. How is her heart even involved already?

Greg pulled into the small shopping plaza parking lot. He pulled right up in front of her studio and put the car in park. There were already four women standing outside the studio with their yoga mats slung over their shoulders. Tessa hit the window button to put her window down.

"Good afternoon, ladies," she said out the window. "Had car troubles. Be right there." She smiled and waved. The women waved back and Tessa put the window back up. "Thank you so much, Greg," she said turning her head to look at him. She wanted him to know she was sincerely thankful for his help. "I can't tell you how much I appreciate you driving me over here, especially with having other obligations."

"Tessa," he said, turning slightly in the driver's seat. "Stop thanking me. I'd do it again... no questions asked. I have my friend towing your VW to his shop to take a look at it. I need your keys so I can drop them off at his place."

"Greg," she said, not recognizing her own voice. Panic and surprise had set in. She was grateful for his generosity, but she was pretty sure she could not afford what was wrong with her car. Basically, she'd just been doing patchwork on it in hopes it would hold out a few more months so she could save up enough money to get a newer used version. "You really didn't have to do that. There's no way I'm going to be able to afford to fix it."

"I'm covering the repairs, Tessa," he said softly. A small smile spread across his lips. "Just give me the keys to the car so I can drop them off. I have Jarod calling me with the estimate and then he can drop the car off to you. We can't have you driving around in a car that's on the verge of breaking down every day. It doesn't sit right with me." His hand came up and stroked the side of her face.

"I don't know what to say," Tessa said. "No one's ever just done something so generous for me. And you don't even know me." She slid her keys out of her purse and wound the VW key off her butterfly keychain. Tessa handed him the key. Greg took the key and set it in the cup holder in the console between them. She looked up at him. His grey eyes were soft and warm as his gaze dropped to her lips. A wave of heat washed over her as the memory of their kiss fluttered through her thoughts.

"I only have one request," he said almost in a whisper. His gaze came back to hers.

"What's that?"

"Go out with me," he said. "Please."

"Like on a date?" she asked shyly.

"Most definitely," he said with a small chuckle. Tessa did everything she could to keep from bursting. This gorgeous man… this generous man wanted to take her out on a date. She knew she would be risking her heart by agreeing to this. How could someone like him really be interested in her? He was a big-time attorney for a large firm making good money and living on the beach. He could probably have any woman he wanted. She was just a young yoga instructor trying to make it on her own. It had taken her three years to save enough money to move out of her mother's rundown bungalow. Her mother would steal money from Tessa for booze and then order Tessa out of the house because she was a bother. She finally had her first apartment. And it wasn't much. Just a little one-bedroom apartment near Tyrone Square Mall. She really had little to offer him besides herself. But he was asking her out.

Even if it was ultimately just sexual, she couldn't find a way to say no to his request. Nothing in her wanted to say no. Just from their limited time together, Tessa knew he was going to open her eyes to a whole new world and that excited her. And that made her want to risk it all.

"It doesn't bother you that I'm twenty-seven?" she asked in all seriousness.

"Does it bother you that I'm forty-two?" he asked. His face was sincere when he asked the question. She could tell he was concerned that his age would be an issue for her.

"Forty-two, huh?" she said, making her best effort to keep a serious tone. "Goodness, you are old! Will you need a walker for the date?" His eyes widened a bit at her comment before she broke into laughter and then so did he.

"So, what are you saying?"

"Yes," she said softly before throwing her arms around his neck. "I say yes." His arm slid around her body and gave her a squeeze. The feel of his hand on her low back sent a heat coursing through her body. She wanted to know what it would be like to feel his hands everywhere on her body. She wanted to throw caution to the wind.

"Good," he said. "I was a little worried you'd say no. Here's my business card." He drew back from her embrace and pulled a card out of the front pocket of his shirt. "It has my cell phone number on it. Call me in two hours and I'll update you about your car and what the plans for tomorrow night will be. I'd make the date tonight, but there's no way I can get out of a client dinner on this short notice. But you're mine for dinner tomorrow!" Tessa took the card from his hand and looked at it.

Gregory T. Snow. Partner. Lowes & Kravitz. She laughed to herself. That card should also say gorgeous and generous and sexy if it were going to be truly accurate.

"Thank you," she said with a smile. "I will call you." She reached for the door handle, but his hand grabbed her forearm and pulled her closer until his forehead touched hers. His grey eyes looked into her own.

"I meant what I said about kissing you," he whispered. His warm breath floated over her face. "I can't wait to do it again." He kissed her on the tip of her nose before pulling back. She sighed. Yep, she sighed. Like nothing in the world could be greater than this moment. "Now get in there and teach those ladies some yoga. I'll talk to you in a bit." Tessa opened her passenger side door and slid from the BMW SUV to the ground. She grabbed her yoga mat and purse from the floor of the car and slung them over her shoulder. "Tessa," Greg called before she shut the door.

"Yes?" She peeked in.

"I can't wait for tomorrow night." A smile spread across his face and Tessa's knees weakened at the look. If he could make her feel this way with just a smile, she was in big trouble. "Enjoy your class." She shut the door and stepped up onto the curb as she watched him drive away.

"Who was that?" one of the girls waiting outside the studio asked. "He's smoking hot!"

"I know," Tessa responded, doing a little dance from where she stood on the curb all the way to the door of her studio. "And he asked me out for tomorrow night."

"Get out!" one of the other girls shouted. "You said yes, right?"

"You better believe it," Tessa said, opening the door of her studio and letting the yogis in. Namaste!

Chapter Three

Greg smiled the entire way back to Advantage. He had watched Tessa in his rearview mirror as he drove away. She danced with what looked like excitement from where he left her until she reached her studio door. He hoped that was a sign that she was as excited as he was about seeing her Saturday night.

He didn't know what came over him at that red light. She just kept talking. He could tell she was nervous, but he didn't know exactly what made her so nervous. He had kept glancing over at her and she just kept talking and gesturing with her hands. It was adorable, but he wanted to put her out of her misery and the only thing he could think to do was kiss her. And it was the best damn decision he had made in days. She had tasted like cotton candy... so sweet. He'd be on this sugar high for the rest of the afternoon. He could have spent the next several hours just kissing her if only they hadn't been at a red light. Oh well, there was always tomorrow.

He had dropped off Tessa's car key at Jarod's, where he had been told the tow truck was already picking up her vehicle, and Jarod promised to get in touch with him within the hour. Greg parked his car in the parking lot at Advantage and walked the relatively short distance to the door. He pulled his pass out of his back pocket and scanned it to gain entrance to the building.

"Mr. Snow," he was greeted by the portly security guard. "Aren't you a little late getting back from lunch?" The guard smiled at him.

"Yes, I am, Sam," Greg said with a smile. "Had a few extra things to do today." Greg walked the short distance through the atrium to the escalator and took it two steps at a time. He was a little over an hour late to the last half of the board meeting. They only met quarterly and he knew he had been running a risk not getting there on time. But something about Tessa called out to him and he didn't regret his decision to be late to the afternoon session one bit. Shit! He had a date with a gorgeous twenty-seven year old yoga instructor. Life didn't get much better than that. He walked towards the executive area and scanned his pass to enter. This place was like Fort Knox.

"Mr. Snow," Suzie McCormick welcomed him pleasantly. She was the executive assistant to Advantage's CEO, Michael Herron, the only inside director on the board. "They just started thirty minutes ago. They held lunch a little longer in hopes you'd be back in time, but none of the men wanted to be here until six on a Friday, so they picked things up just a bit ago." She swept her blonde hair over her shoulder and smiled at him.

Suzie had had an eye for John Dorsey for the last year, but since John got together with Elizabeth, one of Advantage's corporate in-house attorneys, six months ago, Suzie was turning her sights to the other two single men sitting on the board. What used to be relentless flirtation with John was now apparently directed at either himself or Mark Olson. Greg and Mark hung out periodically and played the occasional round of golf on the weekends. They'd spent a few minutes here or there teasing the hell out of each other as to who should nail Suzie and just put her out of her misery.

But in all honesty, Greg wasn't interested in Suzie. Not that she wasn't attractive. She was… in a runway-model-type way. Suzie was tall and slim with beautiful blonde hair and blue eyes. Definitely more Olson's type. Greg had always been attracted to shorter women. His ex-wife had been all of five feet three inches tall and built strong. She'd been crazy beautiful with long blonde hair and bright green eyes. So, Suzie wasn't really his type. And now that he had a date with Tessa, he wasn't even contemplating the alternative. But he knew Mark was not opposed.

He quietly pushed through the large wooden doors to the boardroom as Elizabeth Wright was standing at the table presenting once again on the construction defect case that three Advantage insureds were involved in. All eyes turned in his direction. Phillip Barker, the chairman of the board, nodded at him with a smile. Phillip was a great guy and he didn't run the type of ship that would get Greg in trouble for being late. A couple of the other members might have been annoyed, but Phillip would be okay.

"Nice of you to join us, Greg," Elizabeth said sweetly. Her long auburn hair was pulled back at the nape of her neck and her emerald green eyes shined. John Dorsey was a very lucky man to have landed her and he knew it.

"I apologize," Greg said, bowing his head at her in greeting. He quickly moved towards his seat next to John and sank into the thick leather chair. "Please carry on."

Elizabeth smiled at him and then winked at John before she continued on with her presentation. It was clear that John must have mentioned to her that Greg had been late because of a woman. John and Elizabeth had been trying to set him up with various women since the two of them had become inseparable. They were eager to go on double dates and take trips with another couple. But none of the dates they had set him up on really panned out. It wasn't that Greg was picky. He always had fun on the dates, but none of them sparked anything more than a pleasant time. He had made the conscious effort to not sleep with any of them either. The women had either been friends of Elizabeth's or women that John knew, so he hadn't wanted to ruin his friendship with either of them.

After Elizabeth's glaring presentation, and a question and answer session involving the lawsuit and ongoing discovery, Elizabeth and her boss, General Counsel of Advantage, Corbin Shaw, left the boardroom. She threw a warm smile in John's direction, who smiled and winked at her. Greg had to admit he had been a little envious of their relationship. John had seen her six months ago when she was first introduced to the board and something in him clicked. He went after her full force. He had told Greg he knew the minute he saw Elizabeth that she would be it for him. Here they were six months later, very much in love and preparing to move into John's beach house together.

"Let's take five minutes," Phil said, clapping his hands together before pressing them to the mahogany table and pushing himself up. "I need to hit the head. But Greg, please don't leave the building. It's just a five minute break." Phil's face broke out into a smile as he headed to the large wooden doors. Everyone else in the room laughed, including Greg.

"So, tell me about her," John said, leaning over the arm of his chair.

"What's to tell?" Greg responded. However, he couldn't keep the smile from spreading across his face at just the thought of Tessa.

"You were an hour late coming back to session," John said. "And you're a stickler for time. Not to mention the fact you moaned in my ear when I called you. So, she must be something special." John twirled his pen between his fingers, waiting for Greg to spill it.

"She is gorgeous," Greg said, softly. He didn't really want Mark Olson involved in their conversation. Since Mark's divorce, he's been on the prowl and looking for "fresh meat" as he called it. Tessa would certainly fall under the category of what he'd been chasing lately and he didn't want Mark anywhere near her. "She's a yoga instructor. Owns her own studio on Treasure Island. In fact, she teaches classes downstairs in the gym a couple days a week. I ran into her in the parking lot. Her car broke down. So, I helped her out. And she agreed to go out with me tomorrow night." The idea of seeing Tessa again made him happier than he'd been in quite some time.

"Do you want Elizabeth and I to go with you to keep the pressure off?" John asked.

"I don't think so," Greg said, looking at his friend. "I don't think there'll be any pressure. Tessa and I are on the same page."

"Tessa, eh?" John teased. "I like the name. So, when do Elizabeth and I get to meet her?"

"Christ, Dorsey," Greg said with a laugh. "I just met her."

"Okay, so next weekend you'll bring her over to my place for dinner. Let's say Saturday at six," John said, patting Greg on the back.

"Do I have a choice?" Greg asked with a chuckle.

"Not really," John said. "Especially after I tell Elizabeth. She's going to be mad I didn't set it up for tomorrow." They just laughed as several of the other board members returned from the break and Phil called the last part of the session to order.

Chapter Four

Tessa scurried around her bedroom in her white lace cheeky underwear and matching strapless bra. Greg was picking her up in fifteen minutes and she had no idea what to wear. When she called him to get an update on the status of her car and their plans for Saturday night, he said he wanted to go somewhere fun because he was restless from sitting in a board meeting all day and schmoozing at a client dinner on Friday. He suggested hitting Gators Café & Saloon on John's Pass. Tessa had been there a few times with some friends, but it had been awhile. It was casual and right on the Intracoastal Waterway. She flipped through several items in her small closet. She was leaning towards a halter dress. She had a light blue and indigo paisley dress that she thought suited her.

Even though it was early October, the Florida temperatures still reached into the low nineties during the day. And the evenings only dipped into the low eighties, so she could get away with a halter dress for another several weeks. She'd bring a shrug just in case.

She pulled the paisley dress off its hanger and slipped it on. Standing before the full-length mirror hanging on the back of her bedroom door, she admired herself in the dress. It was flattering to her figure, which was short and leanly muscular with a small chest. Of all the things her mother could pass down to her, she wished it had been to be more fully endowed the way she was. Regardless, the halter dress made it seem like she had more than she did, as did the push up bra. Tessa smiled at herself. Her curly blonde hair fell past her shoulders and the light blue and indigo of the dress made her eyes even bluer. To herself, she looked a little older than her twenty-seven years and that made her happy.

The knock on the door startled her. Greg was here. Oh God! What would he think of her small place? What would he think of her? Her hands brushed over her dress one last time before she walked to the door of her apartment. She peered through the peephole to see Greg standing in the hallway with a bouquet of fresh flowers. Her heart began to race. He looked delectable. A pair of dark jeans with a snug grey t-shirt that clung to his every muscle. She could feel the dampness in her panties already.

"Are you going to open the door?" she heard him say. "I can see your eye in the peephole." Oh shoot! She unlocked the deadbolt and opened the door. He froze and his gaze scanned over her... top to bottom and back to the top. Tessa felt her body flush as he thoroughly took in every inch of her. "Definitely worth the wait," he said, before handing her the flowers.

"Thank you," she said shyly, bringing the flowers to her nose and inhaling their beautiful scent. "Come in." She turned in the doorway and he followed her through, closing the door behind them. Tessa walked the few feet to her small kitchen. Opening the cabinet under the sink, she pulled out a clear glass vase and filled it with water while Greg looked around her apartment.

"So, everything turned out okay with your car?" Greg asked, watching her in the kitchen.

"Yes, thank you so much. I don't know how I'll ever repay you," Tessa replied. "Jarod dropped it off early this morning good as new. I was able to make my morning classes without catching the bus." Placing the flowers in the vase, she set it on the counter between the kitchen and the dining area. "They're beautiful," she whispered. Greg made short distance of the space between them and pulled her body against his. His hands rested at her low back.

"Not nearly as beautiful as you," he said before lowering his mouth to hers. Tessa moaned softly at the feel of his lips on hers again. Greg's lips nimbly worked hers, coaxing her to open up and accept him. And she did. The feel of his tongue slipping into her mouth and mingling with her own was exquisite. And he tasted amazing. Not the caramel coffee of earlier, but rather something minty and fresh. Her hands gripped his grey t-shirt as she held on for dear life. The kiss lasted for several minutes and Tessa was completely breathless when it ended.

"Christ, I've been waiting for too long to do that again," Greg said softly. He kissed her on the forehead and the nose. But Tessa had other ideas. This man turned her inside out and one kiss was not enough to start the evening. Her grip on his t-shirt tightened and she pulled him back to her lips. This time she took some control over the kiss. Her tongue flicked over his lips and then between his lips and into his mouth. The growl that escaped him only encouraged her. One hand moved from his shirt to the back of his neck and up into his short hair. His hold on her low back tightened as she deepened the kiss. Grabbing her hips, he lifted her onto the edge of her countertop and pushed his body between her legs. The fabric of her dress rode up her thighs, and she could feel his erection pressed against her core. Tessa gasped and pulled back from the kiss.

"Greg," she whimpered, looking into his heated grey eyes.

"Don't stop, Tessa," he said roughly. His arousal was apparent in his voice. Weaving his fingers into her curly mane and bending forward, Greg slammed his lips against hers. His hand flexed at the back of her head, holding her in exactly the position he wanted her. And he kissed her senseless, his tongue licking the inside of her mouth as if it couldn't get enough of her. Tessa lost all sense of control. Both hands slid into his hair and pulled him even more into her. Her hips pushed off the counter and ground against his hips. He rubbed his erection against the center of her, hitting her clit with each stroke. With her one hand resting against the countertop, she threw her head back, breaking their kiss. She didn't recognize the mewling sounds that escaped her, but she didn't care. This man knew how to use his body to please her and she was sure she was going to come fully clothed upon her countertop from his shameless efforts.

"Oh God," Tessa cried out. The wave of an orgasm crashed over her and her body shuddered as she splintered into a million pieces. Her hand once again gripped his shirt for support in order to keep herself upright. And Greg still rubbed himself against her, making sure to let her ride out the full wave of ecstasy.

"Fuck, Tessa," he said, nuzzling into her neck as she slowly came down from the high. "That was amazing. I want so desperately to touch you. To taste you. To be inside of you." Tessa stared into his eyes. Now, his face was flushed. She knew that he was worked up. She could feel it between her legs. She slid her hand down the length of her body to the edge of her dress. His gaze followed the path of her fingers as they slipped under her dress. She slid her panties to the side and slipped her middle finger between her wet folds. "Tessa," he growled. But before he could say anything else, she pushed her finger into her sex and moaned. He gripped the countertop so tightly his knuckles turned white. Removing her finger from her wet pussy, she offered it to him.

"Taste me," she said with a confidence she didn't know she had. His gaze never left hers. The heat in his eyes… the heat of his mouth around her finger made her heady. And she knew there was no turning back. He was about to stake his claim on her and she had never wanted anything more in her life.

Chapter Five

Holy fuck! Watching Tessa finger herself then offer him a taste almost made him come in his pants. He truly was so close, and she tasted divine, a spicy feminine flavor that he planned on enjoying more thoroughly. He pulled her hips to the very edge of the counter and lowered onto his haunches. The exhilarating scent of her hit him and made his cock unimaginably harder. He spread her legs farther apart and hooked her panties around two of his fingers to move them out of the way. Fuck! She was a true blonde! Her pussy was covered in short, soft, blonde hairs. His thumbs separated her lips and he growled at the sight of the soft pink flesh, his mouth watering.

"Greg," she pleaded. His gaze rose to hers. Her head was bent forward. Her hands gripped the countertop.

"Tessa, you told me to taste you and I have every intention of doing so," he whispered against her inner thigh as he kissed his way up. "Every intention." As he reached the apex of her legs, his tongue flicked out and over her clit. She practically shot off the counter. Holding her legs down and apart, he lapped up her sex and between her folds, taking his time to taste every part of her. He gave particular attention to that little bundle of nerves that he planned to use to set her off again.

"That feels amazing," she said breathless. "I've never... Oh God!" He watched as her head went back and her breathing became even more erratic. He kept his gaze on her as his mouth closed around her clit and he sucked on it. "Fuck!" she yelled. He groaned against her. He had yet to hear her say a true swear word so it was a turn-on to hear her use one in the midst of pleasuring her. Her body trembled, her legs quaked. Sliding a finger inside her wet pussy, he felt it clamp down and pull him deeper. Christ, she was incredibly tight! The thought of her covering his cock was beyond comprehension. The way she gripped his finger told him she'd be like a second skin on him and his cock throbbed against the fly of his jeans. He watched as her head came forward, her eyes closed tight, and her breath came out in short pants.

"Look at me, Tessa," he ordered, flicking his tongue against her clit and fucking her with his finger. "I want you to know who is making you feel this way." Her eyes opened slowly. He noticed the lusty haze in her eyes as his tongue continued to assault her clit. He felt the quiver of her cunt around his finger and he observed as she crested over the edge.

"Ohhhh," she cried, thrusting her pelvis up. Her hand gripped the back of his head and held him against her until her body started to relax. When she finally sighed, he pulled himself up to his feet and slipped his finger free of her body. Leaning over the counter to where she had slumped in relief, he pressed his lips, moist with her juices, against her mouth.

"I could taste you all night long," he whispered against her lips.

"I'm pretty sure I couldn't survive you doing that all night long," she whispered back. He felt her smile against his lips. "I've never had a man give me an orgasm… let alone two so close in proximity." Greg pulled back from their soft kisses.

"What?" he asked, hearing the worry in his voice. "Are you a virgin, Tessa?" The thought brought back the reality of their age difference. She was twenty-seven. Though he didn't know how men weren't throwing themselves at her, he supposed it was possible that she was not sexually active... that she was a virgin. Tessa laughed.

"Not in the true sense of the word," she said. "I've had sex with a few guys. They just never got me off." Greg felt an unfamiliar feeling rise up inside of him. It was a mixture of jealousy of the guys that had been there before him and anger that those guys hadn't taken care of her.

"So these guys you've been with just got themselves off?" he asked, trying to disguise his anger at the idea. "They didn't touch you? They didn't taste you?" What kind of guy just shoved his dick inside of her without any concern for her comfort or pleasure? Fuck, that pissed him off!

"No one has ever gone down on me before," she said, shaking her head. "But that was amazing. Oh my God! Amazing!" Her blue eyes were big and looking at him in wonderment. "I could get used to that." He watched as a slight blush flowed across her face at this admittance. She was so fucking adorable.

"Oh, Tessa, you better get used to it," he said, smiling at her. "I plan on doing that to you every single chance I get." She gasped as he picked her up from the counter and kissed her on the lips before setting her on the ground. "Do you want to freshen up before we go? We do have a date to go on."

"What about you?" she asked sweetly. "Can I take care of you?" She pushed her tight little body against his and he felt his cock immediately spring to life.

"There's plenty of time for that," he replied, running his fingers through her hair and tilting her head up to look at him. "Go get your shoes and your purse and let's go get something to eat." He placed a small kiss on the tip of her nose before turning her around and slapping her firmly on the behind.

"I'll make you pay for that," she yelped, looking over her shoulder at him as she headed into her bedroom. He saw the heat in her eyes and his cock pressed tightly against his jeans. He realized that he was so sexually on edge right now that anything she did was going to be sheer torture.

Chapter Six

"I know it's a little late for this question given the events back at my apartment and the fact that we sit here on a date eating dinner, but you aren't married, are you?" Tessa asked sheepishly. She felt ridiculous asking the question. She had been spread eagle on top of her kitchen counter with his face buried between her legs only an hour ago. The memory of his eyes looking up at her as he swiped and curled his tongue all over her wet slit caused heat to course through her. He had demanded that she watch him. It hadn't been a request. It was a demand. And that vision would be seared in her memory forever. She'd never experienced anything so erotic.

"Tessa," he said, throwing his head back and laughing a deep belly laugh. "Good God, you are the most adorable thing I've ever laid eyes on." His hand reached out for hers across the table and he entwined their fingers. He looked her straight in the eyes. "No, I'm not married."

"I had to ask," she said softly. "I'm sorry. It's just that I dated a guy for a couple of weeks before I found out he was married. I'm usually a little paranoid about it, but I guess I just got so swept up in you that I was afraid to ask. Afraid of the answer." They had spent the last forty-five minutes eating dinner, sipping drinks and talking about all sorts of things. She learned a little about his parents and two younger brothers and the fact that he grew up in the Sarasota area. She found out that he went to the University of Florida for undergrad and law school. He was interesting to talk to and he was interested in what she had to say, though she had been successful in steering the conversation away from her own family. Her family basically consisted of herself and her drunken mother. She'd never met her father. In fact, she wasn't entirely sure who he might be. And her mother was always too far into the bottle to ever have had another child to care for.

"You don't have to apologize," he said, giving her hand a little squeeze. "I'm not that kind of guy. I never cheated on my ex-wife. And I'd never do that to you." Tessa's eyes widened at his use of the word "ex-wife." She knew there was no way she was the first woman to claim him, but the idea that he had earlier promised his life to a woman made her a bit jealous.

"Ex-wife?" she said, drawing out the words.

"Yes, Tessa, I was married," he said. He brought his pint of beer to his lips and took a sip of the dark brew. "I married Nicole when I was twenty-two. Right out of college. We graduated at the same time, and we married the summer between undergrad and law school for me."

"Why did you divorce?" she asked. Curiosity had gotten the best of her. Tessa didn't know how much of his previous marriage she wanted to know about, but she couldn't stop herself from digging deeper.

"I'm pretty sure I never would have divorced. I took my vows seriously. She asked for it," he replied. He took another sip of his beer and his gaze fell to his pint. But Tessa couldn't do anything but hold on to his hand tighter. Was he still in love with his ex? "The years of marriage through law school weren't so bad. She worked as an accountant for a small firm in Gainesville as I worked my way through law school. But afterwards, I took a job with Lowes & Kravitz in St. Petersburg. I wanted to be a little closer to my parents. And her family was in Fort Myers. She was pissed that I didn't want to stay in Gainesville, but I wanted to be closer to the water. Christ, Florida is all about the beaches and sunsets, right?" Tessa nodded in agreement. She couldn't imagine living anywhere where the beach was more than twenty minutes away.

"But she eventually agreed to move with me. We got a small house just outside of the city limits and Nicole found a job at an accounting firm in the city. I was just an associate at the law firm and I had to work twelve and fourteen hour days... sometimes seven days a week. She started to hate me. I had made her move to a city where she knew no one and then worked my ass off until all I wanted to do was pass out when I got home." He looked back up at her and his eyes were sad. "We fought almost constantly for two years until she finally asked me for a divorce. She just told me she couldn't take being in the marriage by herself."

"I'm sorry," Tessa said. She had no idea what to say.

"I tried to convince her that it would just be another couple years of these hours and then I'd be partner and things would slow down. I'd have more free time. But I think by that time, she was seeing someone else... someone from her accounting firm. And even though I had taken my marriage vows very seriously, I could already tell I'd lost her. So, I didn't fight it." Tessa's heart ached for him. He was unbelievably handsome and sweet and sexy, and it seemed like he had really been heartbroken.

"And so you decided to just stay single?" she asked quietly. She needed to know if he had given himself in that way to anyone else.

"I decided to put my job first," he said smiling at her as if he knew exactly what she was asking. She felt her heart rate accelerate. What he did to her with just a smile baffled her. "Until now." He brought her hand up to his lips and pressed a kiss against the back of her hand.

Tessa slid out of her side of the booth and into the side where Greg sat, all the while still holding his hand. She never wanted to let him go. She tucked her leg underneath her bottom and pushed up to press her lips to his. He moaned against her lips and she took that as an invitation to deepen the kiss. She thrust her tongue into his mouth. He tasted of dark beer and a hint of the blackened spice from his grouper he had eaten for dinner. It was an interesting and exotic blend for her. His hands gripped the sides of her face and he licked deep into her mouth, tangling his tongue with hers.

"Tessa," he moaned. Her hand ran down his chest, feeling his hard muscles underneath. God, she wanted this man to be real... more than anything. She slid her hand further down to the waistband of his jeans until she could feel his erection against her hand. He was rock solid and straining against his jeans. She wanted to unleash him and take him in her mouth... right there. Her fingers started to unbuckle his belt, but his hand grabbed hers. "Stop, Tessa!" he said, breaking their kiss and placing a gentle kiss on her forehead before looking her in the eyes. "I've been on the edge of exploding for a while now. And I don't want to do that until I'm deep inside your beautiful body."

"Then we need to get out of here now," she whispered. "Because I want to make you come more than I want anything else right now." The look of shock on his face, though brief, made her giggle.

"Fuck," he said, shifting to take his wallet out of his back pocket. He pulled out three twenties and threw them on the table before scooting her out of the booth. He grabbed her hand and quite literally dragged her through the front door and into the parking lot. It was a gravel and shell lot and with her wedges on, she had to grasp his bicep to keep her balance.

The sun had set a little over an hour ago and twilight had fallen. The air was filled with saltiness and moisture clung to her skin from the still high humidity. When they reached his BMW at the edge of the lot, he spun her around and pressed her back against the passenger side door. He caged her in with both of his hands on either side of her shoulders. She had just enough time to look up at him and see the lust in his gaze before he slammed his mouth down on hers and kissed her like she was his source of oxygen... like he needed her to live. One of his hands slid down her side and over her hip. He cupped her ass and pulled her into him.

"Do you feel that?" he asked between licks into her mouth. "Do you feel what you do to me?"

"Yes," she whimpered. He felt huge and harder than granite against her abdomen. He was obviously bigger than any guy she had been with and the thought did frighten her a little. Though she wasn't a virgin, she also wasn't very experienced and she'd never been fucked with such a large one... of that she was sure.

"I'm going to fuck you fast and hard the second we get inside my place, but once I release this fucking tension, I'm going to spend the rest of the night making you scream my name. Do you understand that? I am going to make you come so many times and fuck you so thoroughly that the only person you will ever remember fucking you will be me. Now, get in the car before I take you right here." He slammed a rough kiss on her lips before opening her door and letting her climb inside. She watched from the passenger seat as he walked around the front of his car. Before he opened his driver's side door, he took a deep breath. He was obviously trying to calm himself. But Tessa had no intention of allowing that. She smiled to herself as he slid into his seat, buckled his seat belt and started the car. He backed out the parking space and headed toward the exit of the parking lot. Turning on the roadway, he started driving towards Gulf Drive in silence.

Tessa slid her hand across the console and onto his leg. His thigh tensed under her hand, but he kept his eyes on the road and both hands gripped the steering wheel tightly. She heard the turn signal click on as they made a left onto Gulf Drive, headed towards what she imagined was his condo. Her hand moved slowly up his thigh until she felt the bulge in his pants. The corners of her mouth slipped up into a smile. She did this to him. She had some pride in that fact. Her hand cupped him through his jeans and he grabbed her wrist.

"Tessa," he pleaded, still keeping his eyes on the road. She unbuckled her seat belt and raised herself up to lick the side of his neck. His growl was primal and his grip on her wrist grew tighter. "Buckle your seat belt," he ordered as he pushed the gas pedal, moving the car through an intersection. Tessa's other hand came around and undid his belt and the button of his jeans. His head went back against the headrest and he groaned. He had to keep a hand on the steering wheel so she knew she had him and he knew it too. Her hand slid beneath his boxer briefs and for the first time she felt his rock hard cock in the flesh. He was even bigger than she imagined, but she swallowed down the panic because she wanted desperately to give this to him.

"I want to taste you now," she whispered against his neck. Her hand freed him from his underwear and her fingers wrapped around his girth. Slowly, she moved her hand up and down his length.

"Jesus Christ," Greg moaned. Tessa lowered her head to hover over the bulbous head of his cock. She had only given one blowjob in her entire life and she wanted to get it right. She wanted to please him like he did her.

His earthy male scent invaded her senses. God, he smelled amazing! Her tongue flicked out over the head of his cock and his salty flavor made her moan. Gripping the base of his cock, she licked the head again.

"I want to release that tension for you," she whispered against the head his cock before her mouth opened and engulfed him.

"Holy fuck," Greg cried. Her tongue swirled around the head and her fist pumped his length. She felt the car swerve but she was oblivious to where they were. Her entire focus was on his pleasure. Her mouth came down his length until her lips came close to her fist. She was surprised by how much of him she could take in the position they were in. She was crouched over the console sucking him deep into her mouth. The car came to an abrupt stop and his hand that was still grasping her wrist released her and he threw the car into park. His hands weaved into her hair, brushing it from the side of her face. Coming up his length with her mouth, her eyes darted up at him. His gaze focused on where he disappeared inside her mouth. He placed a little pressure on the back of her head and she slid her mouth back down his hard cock until she felt him at the back of her throat.

"That's it, Tessa. Suck me. Take all of me," he said. His voice was rough and gravelly. "Oh fucking Christ, I'm gonna come." His fingers tightened in her hair and he tried to pull her up, but Tessa wanted to taste him... all of him. She worked her mouth up and down his length feeling how it became inconceivably harder the closer he got. The vein on the underside of his cock pulsed against her tongue and his hips pushed up slightly from his seat. The first spurt of cum caught her a bit off guard, but she quickly swallowed it. "Fuuuuuck! Oh God! Yes!" He flooded her mouth with more than she could handle. She felt it spill out of her mouth and run down her chin, but she didn't care. She continued to suck and lick his throbbing cock until she had taken every last drop of him.

When his body finally relaxed into the seat, she pulled herself up to look at him, wiping her mouth with the top of her forearm. His head rested against the back of his seat. His eyes were closed. His breathing was still labored. He looked incredibly handsome when he was completely sated. She wanted to be the reason he had this look on his face all the time. She leaned over and kissed his lips gently.

"Are you still with me?" she asked.

"I don't know," he said with a chuckle. "That was fucking amazing! Seriously!" He opened his grey eyes and looked at her like she was some sort of goddess... some ethereal creature. "Come here," he said pulling her over the console and into his lap. His arms wrapped around her and she pressed her head into his shoulder. It felt amazing to be wrapped up in his arms. She felt safe. She felt cared for. Dare, she say it... she felt loved. "Thank you," he whispered into her ear. "Now, I can relax when I make love to you." She shivered in his arms at his words, but she snuggled as close to him as she physically could.

Chapter Seven

Greg was pretty sure he had just died and gone to heaven and that this beautiful woman he held in his arms was some sort of heavenly creature. Good God, he'd never had a blowjob like that! He had been so worked up since meeting her that he had actually been a little afraid that he would hurt her. That's how bad he wanted her. He knew he was going to come hard, but she took it… every last bit of him.

They had been lucky he only lived a mile or so from Gator's because if he had to drive any further, he may have wrecked the Bimmer. Pulling into his condo property, he had slammed the car into the first open space so that he could enjoy her sensuous mouth and what it did to him. Just the thought of her warm mouth swallowing his dick made him almost hard and ready to go again.

Tessa snuggled into him and he held her tight. He didn't want her to feel used because that was so far from the truth. This woman had turned him inside out. He wanted to give her the world. And he had just met her. It seemed like there was something broken in her and he couldn't quite figure it out. She was definitely tight-lipped about her family. But he wanted to make everything right in her world. And he had to admit, it was nice to be needed again. He missed having a woman to care for.

"Mansions on the Gulf?" she whispered. Her head lifted from his shoulder as she looked around and saw the property sign.

"Yes, my place is at the top of that building," he replied, pointing in the direction of a tan building with balconies all the way around it. "The name's a little pretentious. The condo association has discussed changing the name, but some of the older members seem to like it. It's beautiful inside. There's a private beach. A large pool. Tennis courts. And a nice bar-slash-café downstairs that is open only to residents and their guests."

"I can't imagine there are a lot of young people that could afford a place in that building," she said.

"Are you implying that I'm not young?" he asked in a joking manner. "Because if that's so, I'm going to put you over my knee when we get up to my place." Her eyes widened at his words, but her bottom squirmed over his lap as if in anticipation of a spanking. "I'm thinking you might like a spanking." He quirked an eyebrow up in a questioning manner.

"I've never had one," she replied. "But I may like it."

"Well then, let's get this car parked in my actual spot and get upstairs. I have a whole night of pleasuring you ahead of me and I don't want to waste another minute sitting in here." He helped her back into the passenger seat and put the car in reverse. He pulled the BMW into a spot a little closer to the building and under cover.

Straightening his pants before he climbed out of his car, he walked over and opened Tessa's door. She took the hand he held out for her and he walked her into the atrium of his building hand in hand.

"Mr. Snow, welcome home," Jack said from behind the security desk. Jack was a sixty-year-old man that had been working security for the Mansions on the Gulf building for the last three years. Greg had taken the time to get to know him a bit. He had a wife and three grown children that were finally producing him grandchildren. Greg enjoyed Jack and his every day pleasantries.

"Thanks, Jack," Greg said. "It's good to be home." He squeezed Tessa's hand. Jack's gaze fell to their joined hands and he raised an eyebrow at Tessa and a small smile sat on his lips. Jack knew that Greg didn't bring women home, at least not on Jack's watch. "This is Tessa. Tessa, Jack." The two shook hands and exchanged nice-to-meet-yous. "Have a great night," Greg said to Jack as he pulled Tessa towards the elevator.

Once inside the elevator, Greg pulled her into him, her back to his front and he kissed the top of her head. She relaxed into him, resting her head against his chest and entwining her fingers with his at her waist. They rode up to his floor in silence.

The elevator doors opened and he pulled her out into the hallway. There were only two condos per floor. The hallway was small and painted a warm neutral with a cherry wood console table against the wall below a gilded mirror. Someone, Greg never really figured out who exactly, would place a fresh flower arrangement on the console table every week. Both doors to the independent condos were solid oak with brass door handles. Greg had always thought it strange how you entered the building and almost felt the décor was more northerly. But the northern flair ended once you walked into his place.

"Oh my God," Tessa said, as he unlocked his oak door and pushed it open to let her in. The kitchen and living room area was basically wide open and had a wall of floor-to-ceiling windows that looked directly out over the Gulf of Mexico. At sunset, it really was an amazing view, but in the darkness of night, it was not as easy to appreciate. "It's like walking into Key West. I love it! It feels so beachy... so coastal. I mean, I know it really is coastal, it being on the coast and all, but you know, some people decorate their places on the islands to look so touristy and well... yours is classy coastal. It's..." Her continued talking was silenced when Greg pushed her against the wall behind her and kissed her senseless.

"I'm beginning to find that this may be the only way to get you to stop talking when you get nervous or flustered," he chuckled against her lips. "Not that I mind or anything." He nipped at her bottom lip and she whimpered.

"I'm sorry," Tessa said softly.

"Don't be sorry," Greg said, pulling back slightly from their kiss and running the back of his hand along her cheek. "I'll always be looking for a reason to kiss you. It just so happens this can be one of them."

"You don't need a reason to kiss me," she replied. Pushing up on her tiptoes, she pressed her lips against his. Her hands snaked around his neck and drew him more into her as she took complete control of the kiss. She bit his lower lip and swallowed the groan that escaped him. Penetrating his mouth with her tongue, she explored every crevice.

Greg's hands wandered down her sides and gripped her ass. He loved the firmness of her backside, the way he could grip it and pull her into him. He pushed his pelvis into her, pinning her against the wall. She may be taking charge of the kiss right now, but he wanted her to know that he had every intention of taking charge of everything else. Her body rubbed up against his erection until he could no longer take it another second. He lifted her in his arms.

"Wrap your legs around me," he said, not recognizing his own voice. It sounded deep and gravelly. Tessa did as she was told. This only made Greg's situation more precarious because now she ground against his erection as she was perfectly positioned. He started the walk down his hallway. Damn it! Why did his bedroom have to be the furthest room down the hall?

"Greg," Tessa panted. He could tell she was getting herself off rubbing against him. Bursting through his bedroom door, he walked up to his king sized bed and tossed her on it.

"Tessa, you're going to kill me," he said, peeling his shirt off over his head and kicking his shoes to the side. "I can't have you coming again without being inside you, and I can't have you making me come until that tight little pussy of yours is wrapped around me." He loosened his belt and undid his jeans, pushing them down to the floor before stepping out of them. He stood before her in just his grey boxer briefs. Her eyes were wide as a doe's as her gaze raked over every inch of his body.

"God, you're beautiful, Greg," she whispered.

He walked over to where she sat on the bed and bent down, placing a soft kiss on her lips while his hands slowly untied her halter dress at her neck. It fell forward to reveal her breasts covered in a white strapless bra. His fingers worked the back of her bra until it fell off and he could see her small perky breasts. They were not big… less than a handful, but they sat at perfect attention and her nipples were rosy and peaked. They were perfect. He leaned forward and took a nipple between his lips, pulling it into his mouth with suction. She arched her back and moaned. His teeth gently bit down on her nipple and she yelped. His mouth moved to her other breast, giving it the same attention.

Pushing her back on the bed, his hands pulled the halter dress down her body and over her hips, revealing her white lace panties. Hooking his thumbs in the side of her panties, he took them with her dress down her legs.

"You are beautiful," Greg said softly as he dropped her clothes to the floor and stood back staring at her sprawled completely naked on his bed. He reached for a condom in his nightstand drawer. Ripping open the foil packet, he sheathed his cock before climbing on the bed. "I don't know what I did to deserve you coming into my life, but I will be forever grateful." His body covered hers. His cock nestled in the warmth between her legs. It took every ounce of strength he had not to sink into her immediately. But this wasn't just about him, especially considering the other men she'd been with didn't seem to care about her pleasure. He planned to make sure she enjoyed every second with him.

His mouth lowered to hers and he kissed her gently. His hands weaved into her long blonde hair while his forearms kept him from crushing her. Her skin was silky smooth against his own. Her body felt amazing pushed against him. He pressed little kisses over her cheeks, her eyes, her nose.

"Make love to me, Greg," she moaned softly. "Please." The sound that escaped him took him by surprise. Hearing her say those words made him lightheaded with desire. He'd been with a few women over the years, but none that made him feel so needed... so wanted.

"I'd love nothing more," he whispered, nibbling on her earlobe. Pushing the head of his cock against her wet slit, he slowly sunk into her a couple of inches. Her eyes clinched shut and her fingernails dug into his biceps, so he froze above her. He wasn't sure how long he could hold off. Her pussy was tight... tighter than he could have imagined. Even with the condom on, he felt extraordinarily snug inside her and he was not nearly as deep as he wanted to be.

"Tessa," he said, sounding breathy. "I'm not hurting you, am I?" God, the last thing he wanted to do was hurt her. He watched as her face softened, her muscles relaxing and as they did, so did the rest of her body.

"Deeper," she gasped, raising her hips just slightly to take a little more of his length. Greg's body stiffened, as did his cock.

"I need to know that I'm not hurting you," he grunted as her hips rotated against him again.

"You're not hurting me," she said, opening her eyes to look at him. "You're big. Really big. I just needed a minute."

"You're good for my ego," he said with a small laugh. "Not only am I about to make love to an incredibly beautiful woman, but she thinks my cock is really big. Can this night get any better?" Tessa giggled and the sound made him unimaginably harder.

"Perhaps I can help you with that. Can you make love to me later?" she asked with a sexy smile. "I really need you to fuck me with that big cock. Right. Now." She raised her hips off the bed and took more of him, making Greg growl like an animal. Her movements and her words were driving him crazy.

"Is that how you want to play this?" he asked, then he slammed into her to the hilt. Holy shit! Jesus Christ! There was no way he was going to last.

"Oh God," she cried as his body took over. The sensation of her tight pussy clamping down on his cock was unbelievable. The sensation of moving in and out of her slick body sent him over the edge and his hips pistoned into her, pinning her to the bed. She threw her head back, arching her neck and cried out. Her pussy tightened even further and then she shuddered as the walls of her cunt pulsed around him. She was so snug that his cock felt every little tremor.

"Fuck, Tessa! Fuck," he said before his own body shuddered and he emptied himself inside her, then collapsed on top of her, making sure to hold up enough of his weight.

He would have thought he was a teenager coming so quickly, so hard. He couldn't remember the last time he had been so aroused, so excited to be with a woman. Sure, he could get a woody with just the idea of sex, but Greg knew he really was a one-woman-type of guy. So, having random sex with someone he saw no future with didn't bring him to the same level of arousal. But he saw a future with Tessa, as crazy as that sounded.

"Wow," she sighed. "That was amazing. You are amazing. Your cock is amazing." She giggled and he pulled back just a bit to watch the flush spread over her at the mention of his cock. He nuzzled into her neck before he started to laugh.

"I'm a bad influence on you," he said against the skin of her neck.

"Why's that?"

"When I first met you yesterday, you were cussing like kindergartener. Now, all I hear is fuck and cock," he said with a laugh.

"True. You are a bad influence on me," she said with a thoughtful tone. "Do you think we can get another round of bad influence in before I pass out?" He pulled his head up from the spot on her neck that he showered with kisses.

"Seriously?" he asked, looking into her blue eyes.

"Seriously," she replied, moving her hips against him. He groaned and felt himself start to stiffen again.

"I haven't even pulled out yet and you're ready to go again?" He ran his fingers along her cheek. His thumb brushed gently over her bottom lip.

"Please," she said with a giggle. He lowered his lips to her and nuzzled her bottom lip between his teeth.

"You're going to be the death of me, Tessa," he whispered against her mouth. "But I can't think of a better way to go than buried inside you." He pulled out of her, tossed her over his shoulder and walked her to the bathroom, where he fucked her in the shower until she was incapable of standing. Then he carried her back to his bed and slept like a log wrapped around her beautiful body.

Chapter Eight

"Start to wiggle your toes," Tessa said softly, sitting on her purple yoga mat at the front of the studio classroom at Advantage. Everyone was in relaxation pose, lying on their backs. "Wiggle your fingertips." She was slowly bringing them back to the present. She was wrapping up her Friday lunchtime class and then had to hustle to her studio for her Friday afternoon class there.

She could hardly believe it had been almost exactly one week since she met Greg in the parking lot of this office building. It had been a glorious week. He'd made a great effort, especially considering his work schedule, to see her every day even if for just for a short while. She had only spent two nights without him. He had to work a couple of nights really late, so he reluctantly agreed to sleep apart. But he had stressed to her that he had not liked it. And the moment he was within ten feet of her, he couldn't keep his hands off of her. He had to be touching her in some fashion.

"Roll over to one side," she said, continuing on with her class. "Please push up to a comfortable seat." The twelve students did as they were told. "Breathe in and raise your hands over your head. Exhale your hands in prayer position." She did as she instructed the class to do. "The spirit in me honors the spirit in you. Namaste." She bowed forward and so did the students. After a few seconds of silence, the students started to rise and roll up their yoga mats.

"Thanks, Tessa," several of the female students said before walking out the door.

"Yeah, Tessa, thanks," said a guy that had been attending her class for the last several weeks. She thought his name was Brad or Brandon or something like that. He was one of three guys that attempted to join the class. She loved having guys in her class because guys were so in need of improving their flexibility. It was nice to see a few guys admit that.

"You're welcome," she said, smiling at him. She squatted and started to roll up her yoga mat. She had noticed that a gorgeous red head was moving slow in gathering her things, sort of lingering. She was new to the class. Tessa had been teaching at Advantage for months now and had never seen her in a class before.

"Tessa," the auburn haired beauty said, walking towards the front of the class where Tessa stood.

"Yes," Tessa said.

"I'm Elizabeth Wright," she said, holding out her hand. "John Dorsey's girlfriend." The name sounded familiar, but Tessa couldn't figure out where she had heard either of their names or why she should know them.

"Nice to meet you, Elizabeth," Tessa said, grasping her hand and shaking it gently. Elizabeth had a firm handshake. It was almost intimidating.

"You don't know who I am, do you?" Elizabeth asked softly. Tessa watched as her green eyes sparkled and a smile inched across her lips.

"Sorry," Tessa said. "Am I supposed to?" Tessa slid her yoga mat over her shoulder and picked up her purse from the floor by the mirrors.

"You and Greg are coming over tomorrow night for dinner at our place on the beach," Elizabeth said. The smile still on her lips. "Well, it's technically John's place. I'm partially moved in."

"Oh God," Tessa said. Now she knew where she had heard the names before. Greg had told her that his friends wanted to have them over for dinner. He had explained that the two of them had been eager for him to get a woman so they could double date and travel together and they were so excited he was dating her. Tessa had been a little worried about the dinner. There was a huge age difference between her and Greg and even though neither of them were bothered by the age gap, she couldn't be sure that his friends would accept her.

"Well, at least now, I know that Greg mentioned the dinner. I was afraid perhaps he didn't tell you in hopes that he might be able to wiggle his way out of it," Elizabeth said with a giggle. She was definitely older than Tessa, but not by much. Elizabeth had no wrinkles, no crow's feet, no laugh lines. And she was gorgeous. Tessa actually felt childlike next to Elizabeth's voluptuous body.

"He did mention it," Tessa said softly.

"Good," Elizabeth continued. "I didn't want to have to kick his ass for trying to keep you to himself. I mean, seriously, John tells me Greg's been MIA since meeting you, which I think is wonderful. Greg is a doll and he deserves a good woman. I thought we'd never find him one and as it turns out, he was capable of finding one on his own." She smiled broadly and winked at her.

Tessa couldn't help but smile herself. Even though Elizabeth looked like a model on the cover of a lingerie magazine, there was something about her that made Tessa like her immediately. Maybe it was the fact that she obviously cared for Greg and seemed to look after him and that made Tessa happy to know that he had good friends. Maybe it was the fact that Elizabeth seemed so excited about meeting her. Maybe it was the prospect of actually having a girlfriend. God knows, it wasn't easy making friends growing up when she had to care for her drunken mother regularly.

"John and I are really looking forward to having you guys over tomorrow," Elizabeth said, resting her hand on Tessa's shoulder. "It will be a good time."

"Thank you," Tessa replied, starting to walk towards the classroom door. "It was sweet of you guys to invite us."

"Ha! As if we'd pass up the opportunity to meet the girl that got under Greg's skin," she said, holding the door of the classroom open for Tessa. "I can't tell you how happy I am that he's found someone that puts such a huge smile on his face. He deserves it."

"Well, it was a pleasure to meet you early, Elizabeth," Tessa said, standing at the doorway of the gym. "I will be so much more comfortable now heading your way tomorrow. Thank you for introducing yourself. I appreciate it."

"Absolutely. Thanks for such a great class. I'll be down here twice a week for sure now. I didn't know what I was missing," Elizabeth said. "See you tomorrow." She threw an arm around Tessa and gave her a quick squeeze before disappearing in the women's locker room.

Tessa wandered out of the building and to her VW Bug in the parking lot. She hadn't had a single issue with her car since Greg had it fixed. In fact, it seemed to be even better on gas mileage and all the squeaks and squeals were non-existent now. She probably owed Greg more than the car was worth given the fact it was a 1998 model, but she did love it, even more so now. That darn car was the reason she met him.

She loaded her things in her car and headed out towards Treasure Island and her studio. About halfway there, her phone started buzzing. She picked it up and saw Greg's name on the screen.

"Hey," she said, answering the phone.

"Hey yourself," he replied. "I just got a phone call from Elizabeth. She said she ambushed you in yoga today and I wanted to make sure you were alright." The concern in his voice warmed her. He really did care about her. She couldn't remember the last time she felt like anyone really cared about her. Her mother only cared whether she had a few bucks for the next bottle of gin.

"I'm fine," Tessa said with a laugh. "I wouldn't necessarily call it an ambush." She cruised down First Avenue North. For whatever reason, traffic was relatively light.

"Elizabeth is really sweet," Greg said. "But she can also be a little overwhelming."

"She caught me off guard, but she was great. I'm actually glad I got to meet her. It takes a little of the edge off of tomorrow night."

"I'm sorry about that," he said softly. "I wouldn't bombard you with my friends this soon if it weren't for the fact that neither of them will take no for an answer."

"Don't worry about it," Tessa replied. "I'm glad you have such good friends."

"They will love you, Tessa," he said. The tone of his voice showed that he knew what her concern was. How did he know her so well already? "How could they not love you? I do." She felt her eyes grow large as she came to a stop at the red light before the bridge. The same spot that Greg first kissed her. The same spot where he just said that he loved her. What the flip is with this red light? Did he just say that? Did he just say he loved her? She sat there speechless.

"Tessa? Tessa, you still there?" she heard Greg say.

"Uh, yes. Yeah," she replied.

"Where'd you go? I thought the call dropped, except I could hear your radio. I asked you about dinner tonight and got no response. You okay?" He sounded completely oblivious to the bomb he dropped a couple minutes ago.

"Yeah. Yeah, I'm great," she said. No matter how hard she tried, she couldn't wipe the ridiculous grin off her face. "Dinner would be wonderful."

"Great. I'll pick you up at seven," he said. "Gotta run. Have a conference call with a big client in five minutes, but I had to make sure Elizabeth didn't have you running for the hills."

"We're in Florida, Greg. There are no hills." She heard him laugh a big laugh.

"Very true. Nonetheless, I'm glad you're still here," he said. She could hear the smile in his voice. "I can't wait to see you later."

"Me too," she said as she pulled into the parking lot of her yoga studio.

Chapter Nine

"They live here?" Tessa asked as Greg pulled his BMW into the driveway into John Dorsey's beach house on Pass-a-Grille beach. It was a three-story Spanish style house with multiple floor to ceiling windows and a tiled roof.

"John's been here for a couple years," Greg said, putting the car in park. "He built it himself. Elizabeth has only lived here for a couple weeks… technically, that is. In fact, I'm not sure all her stuff is even here yet." He looked over at her in the passenger seat and winked.

Tessa looked adorable. She wore a little black dress and her hair was pulled back in a knot at the nape of her neck with wisps. With her hair off her neck, Greg had a difficult time not staring at the elegant length of it. On more than one occasion since picking her up, he had to convince himself not to lean over and run his tongue along her skin from her collarbone to that delicate spot just under her ear. Quite honestly, he could not get enough of her.

They had dinner last night at a sophisticated restaurant up the coast on Madeira Beach. He stayed the night at her place because she had class in the morning and refused to drive his BMW. But that was fine. He didn't really care where they stayed so long as he could spend the night making love to her and waking up next to her in the morning to make love to her again. Those few days they had stayed at their own places had been excruciating. Greg knew they hadn't known each other long, but he wanted to spend every moment he could with this woman.

"Your expression is even more hysterical than when you first saw where I lived," Greg said, leaning over the console and kissing her cheek. "Let's go. Elizabeth is sure to be awaiting our arrival."

"I can't believe how far out of my element I am here," she said quietly. Her gaze raised to his and he saw worry in her eyes.

"What is it, Tessa?" he asked. He held her chin between his forefinger and thumb.

"We're from different worlds," she said softly. He could see the tears welling up in her eyes.

"What makes you say that?" He scanned her face. The beat of his heart increased as he wasn't sure where this conversation was headed. A tear escaped her eye and ran down the side of her face. He leaned forward and kissed it away.

"Look at this place. I have no fantasy that this is the kind of place I'd ever live. I'm a yoga instructor, for flipping sake. Look at where you live! Not to mention the fact that I'm twenty-seven and well…you're not. We're just on different planets."

"Tessa, I will move to whatever planet you want to live on. I don't care where we are." He felt himself start to panic. After his divorce from Nicole, he buried himself in his work. He didn't know if he'd ever really put himself back out there… until he met Tessa. She put a chink in his armored heart and now he feared she was about to end it all.

"You're too good for me," she said, looking him in the eyes. "I'm an only child, who has no idea who her father is. I've never met him. And my mother is an alcoholic of epic proportions. I've taken care of her for years despite the fact that she has stolen from me, beat me down both physically and emotionally. I'm finally on my own and making a go of my life. I can't afford to fall head over heels in love with you only to have my heart shattered. I can't do it, Greg. This whole relationship is going to blow up in our faces." He had known there was something in her that was broken. And now that he knew what put those insecurities in her head, he promised himself he would not stop until she felt completely secure in his love for her.

"You know what, Tessa," he said. "You're right. This may blow up in our faces. It may. But then again, I think I'm more likely to change your name." Her eyes grew round as saucers. She looked like a doe in headlights.

"What are you saying?" she asked. He could hear the quiver in her voice. He took her hands in his and brought them to his lips, pressing little kisses over them.

"I'm saying I'm going to marry you," he said, watching her reaction carefully. "I'm saying I want to give you my name. I want to take care of you. I want to laugh with you, cry with you. I want to love you. I most definitely want to make love to you over and over again. I know that we have only known each other for a very short time, but the minute I saw you, my heart opened up again. So, please don't break up with me. Please give this… give us a chance."

"Oh. God," she said, tears streaming down her face. He gripped the back of her head and pulled her closer to him. Leaning his forehead against hers, he looked deep into her eyes.

"Please give me a chance," he pleaded.

"Yes. Yes. Yes!" she said through her tears and pressed her lips against his. Her hands came up and cupped his face as she deepened the kiss. The feel and taste of her tongue surging into his mouth made him moan in hunger and he wished they were anywhere but sitting in the driveway of his good friends' house because he wanted more than anything to make love to her right now.

"Hey! Are you going to come in for dinner or are you going to spend the evening making out in my driveway?" he heard Dorsey say as he banged on the driver's side window.

"Oh flip," Tessa said, ducking her head in embarrassment.

"I told you we should have gone in right away," he said, placing a kiss on her nose. "These two can't keep their nose out of my business." He heard her giggle. Greg rolled down his window just a crack. "Get your ass back into your house. We'll be in in a minute. You need to work on your patience."

"Ha-ha! Elizabeth wanted me to come out here the second you pulled in the driveway. Consider yourself lucky you got the minutes you did," John said over his shoulder as he turned and walked back towards his front door.

Greg looked over at Tessa, who was fixing herself in the mirror on the shade. He watched as she powdered away her tearstains and spread lip-gloss over her beautiful lips.

"You know I'm just going to kiss that off you, right?" he asked. She looked over at him and smiled. Her blue eyes sparkled and her smile was genuine, reaching her eyes. Damn! He was one lucky son of a bitch.

"Well, I certainly hope so," she whispered in her sexy voice. She popped open her door and hopped out of the BMW. "Let's go start the colliding of our worlds," she said, leaning back into the passenger side as he sat there almost dumbfounded. She slammed the door shut and started walking the short distance to the front door, shimmying her backside the entire way. He groaned. He was going to have to take her over his knee soon because she obviously enjoyed torturing him way too much.

He watched as Tessa was greeted immediately by Elizabeth and John. Elizabeth enveloped her in a warm embrace before Greg could even get out of his car. He received the same welcome from Elizabeth.

"I really like her, Greg," Elizabeth whispered in his ear. "You're both very lucky to have found each other. John and I approve." He followed the three of them into the house to the smell of some delicious Italian dinner. He smiled broadly as he sipped on his glass of Chianti and watched Tessa carry on with his friends. He really was a lucky man.

The End

DEDICATION

To Stacie, Natalie & Chris—my beta readers and truth-tellers. Thank you! Without your insight and suggestions, this story wouldn't be nearly as complete.

To my husband—thank you for all the encouragement to carry on with this story despite the multiple obstacles.

To the guys at LC Technology—THANK YOU! Thank you for saving me and recovering this story (and others)!

TAKING ADVANTAGE

BOARD INDISCRETION

Taking Advantage, 3

Jessica Jayne

Copyright © 2014

Chapter One

"Whiskey. Neat," Mark Olson said to the bartender. The dark-haired twenty-something guy behind the bar nodded at Mark as he bellied up to the Beach Club bar for the second night this weekend. Friday night, his visit had been a last minute decision after finishing his work at his car dealership in Tampa. On most normal days, he worked out of his St. Petersburg location because it was closer to where he lived on St. Pete Beach, but with a new manager at his Tampa dealership, Mark needed to supervise the transition. After all, this was his livelihood. Lord knew with the monthly alimony to his ex-wife and child support payments for his two daughters, Angela and Laura, he couldn't afford to have an issue with one of his three locations. His girls were ten and twelve years old respectively. College wasn't that far off anymore.

"Running a tab?" the bartender asked. Mark nodded. The bartender slid the tumbler with the amber liquid across the bar. Wrapping his fingers around the glass, Mark brought it to his lips. The whiskey fumes infiltrated his nose, bringing with it the familiar burn that would soon be gliding down his throat and into his belly. He nodded at the bartender to let him know the pour was right before taking his first sip of his favorite vice.

Mark was a familiar face at the Beach Club on St. Pete Beach. Almost every Saturday night, he stopped in for a few drinks and often found himself leaving with a hot female to cure his other vice...getting laid. He'd been divorced for almost three years now and he'd added more notches to his belt since those papers were signed than he cared to count. Spending almost fifteen years with a woman that looked at sex like it was a chore, he couldn't seem to get enough of sticking his dick in any warm-blooded woman that appeared interested.

He took another sip of his whiskey and sighed. That was, he used to have a new woman every weekend to remedy his cravings. Lately, however, one woman and one woman alone had permeated his thoughts and his desires. And it seemed only she could feed his hunger. Suzannah McCormick.

Since his divorce, he'd convinced himself that remaining single was what he wanted. It made things less complicated for his two pre-teen daughters. *Shit!* It made things less complicated for himself. But that lifestyle could also be quite lonely.

That's where Suzie came in and complicated the hell out of his life. She was the executive assistant to the CEO of Advantage Insurance Company, Michael Herron, and well... Mark was a member of Advantage's board of directors, had been for several years. He loved his position on the board. Aside from the small amount of prestige it carried, he'd made great friends with the other members, particularly the two younger board members—John Dorsey and Greg Snow. A relationship with Suzie could compromise his position on the board and with the members, but truth be told, he also loved his most recent position between her legs.

If only the situation was different.

A familiar giggle wafted in from the direction of the dance floor. The delicate sound stirred his cock to life. It stiffened against his black trousers instantly. After several weeks of clandestine meetings involving dirty talk and hard fucks, he'd know that giggle anywhere. He'd heard it many times afterwards when they lay tangled in each other's limbs. Turning his head in the direction of the dance floor, anger heated his face and his hands clenched into fists on the bar top at the sight he witnessed.

Sandwiched between two guys that he'd now refer to as dickheads, danced the woman that wreaked havoc on his single life status. Her little black dress clung to her trim frame, emphasizing her small, but very perky breasts and showing off her figure that could easily grace the cover of any fashion magazine. Her legs stretched for miles and her creamy white skin contrasted nicely against the jet black of her dress. Flinging her silky blonde hair over her shoulder and down her back, her pink Pursecase carrying her iPhone dangled from her wrist as her hips gyrated against her two dance partners. The taller man dancing behind her slipped his hand over her hip and rested it over her low belly as he rubbed what Mark was sure to be a rock hard erection against Suzie's ass.

What the fuck is she doing?

First, she never came to the Beach Club. Never. In all his regular visits to this club over the last couple of years, he had yet to see her in here once. Not once! Second, she was practically dry-humping two guys in the middle of the dance floor. That wasn't her typical style.

Suzie was one of those beautiful women that appeared to have the girl-next-door innocence. She didn't dress too provocatively. She was sexy, but in that way that was just natural. Her bubbly Southern charm won over all the men on the board of directors and Mark speculated it would win over anyone. He flirted with her, teasing her on board days to get a rise out of her. There'd always been a twinkle of mischief in her eyes when he flirted with her that would leave him questioning whether he knew her at all.

At last quarter's board meeting, she left him dumbfounded when she responded to his flirtation with a proposition. After mulling it over for a bit, which actually had turned out to be a couple weeks, he called her bluff. He asked her over to his place for cocktails and she showed up. What he learned was that there was a lot more to Suzannah McCormick than met the eye. The rest was history.

Throwing back the last remnants of his whiskey, he stood from his stool, tossed some cash on the bar, and turned toward the dance floor. He wrestled with what his next move should be.

He refused to let her talk about a relationship with him because of his position on the board of directors at Advantage, but watching her dancing with those two assholes pissed him off.

Fuck if he was going to let some other guy touch her while he was standing right here.

His long stride made short distance of the space where he stood and she danced. Her head rolled back and to the side, her blue eyes stopping when she noticed he stood mere inches from her writhing body.

"Mark!" Her body stilled despite the fact the two guys continued to undulate against her.

"Excuse me, fellas." Mark grabbed her by the wrist. "I'm cutting in." He pulled her free from the two men, who protested over the loud music of the cover band.

"Dude, get your own girl," the shorter guy said, clearly inebriated and puffing up like a rooster ready for a cock fight. His taller buddy wrapped an arm around his friend and dragged him off toward the bar, recognizing this wasn't a battle either of them wanted to fight.

"Fuck off," Mark said before they got too far. The short guy turned around and flipped him the middle finger, but his friend seemed to maintain control of him, so Mark let it go. His hands gripped Suzie's hips harshly, his fingers digging into her flesh. His narrowed eyes met hers, issuing her a warning that his temper was flared.

"Funny running into you here," she said. Her breath warmed the side of his face as it fanned across his cheek. God damn if his cock didn't twitch against his zipper at the sound of her breathy voice.

"What brings you here, baby?" The harshness in his voice didn't go unnoticed as her eyes widened. He pulled her body hard against his, causing a small gasp to escape her lips when she felt his arousal against her pelvis. The fact that she was surprised by her effect on him astounded him. He'd been unable to keep his hands off her since their first secret meeting at his place.

"I'm just looking for a little fun," she said. Her beautiful blue eyes glistened with mischief and her mouth curved up on one side into a devilish grin that made him impossibly harder. *Damn, she is beautiful.* "I missed you."

"You missed me? Or my cock?" he whispered close to her ear. Her face flushed at the mention of the part of him that had brought her numerous orgasms over the last several weeks. Color always looked good on her.

Her naturally creamy skin blushed beautifully, especially her ass.

"Would it be wrong of me to say both?" She looked at him through her eyelashes.

"There is little you could say that would be wrong, baby." He ran a finger along her jaw line. She shuddered at his touch and he couldn't help but feel pride over the effect he had on her. "This isn't your usual hangout." His words weren't a question, but she responded anyway.

"I've never been here," she said. "I was hoping you might be."

Because of their situation, up to this point, their rendezvous had been planned. They met at his place after hours when he didn't have his girls.

He didn't want to resign from the board. Even more so, he hadn't wanted to risk her job. Suzie was good at her job. Her boss, Michael, raved about her, and the other board members loved her too. The agendas were always ready to go. iPads were set up with the Power Point presentations loaded. Coffee and water was readily available. Her pleasant demeanor and great sense of humor made for enjoyable board days every quarter. Not to mention all of the work she did keeping Michael in line and at the right meetings every day. Advantage and its CEO would be at a loss without her.

Apparently, she made the decision on her own to up the stakes of their situation.

"You were hoping I might be here?" He weaved a hand into her long hair and pulled it slightly to get her full attention. "And yet, you didn't approach me at the bar. Rather, you dry fucked two assholes on the dance floor." He paused. "If I didn't know any better, I'd guess you're trying to make me jealous." His voice was stern.

He had feelings for Suzie, of that he couldn't deny. She'd turned him on, always had, from the moment he walked through the doors of Advantage's executive suite and saw her sitting at her desk outside the CEO's office. But he didn't enjoy games. That was one of the main reasons he decided to stay away from any sort of relationship since the failure of his marriage. Women were full of games in an effort to land a man, especially a man who had done well for himself. Mark fell into that category with three dealerships between Hillsborough and Pinellas counties.

Was he being fair to her? That question crossed his mind on more than one occasion. He couldn't really give her anything more than their secret meetings and yet, he didn't want her with anyone else. He'd thought a few times of ending their relationship, but the idea always caused his chest to tighten and he just couldn't bring himself to tell her they had to stop seeing each other. Even now, thinking that she was toying with him in an effort to get a rise out of him, he'd normally walk away, but he couldn't. And yet, he couldn't commit to her either.

Yep! He was a certified asshole.

Chapter Two

"Are you jealous?" Suzie asked. Her gaze searched Mark's face, looking for a hint of emotion, as they swayed on the dance floor at the Beach Club. His lips drew in a thin line and his brow furrowed. Then she saw it. A little flicker of something—was it jealousy?—swept through his eyes.

"If you're asking me if I like to see another man's hands on you, then the answer is no," His voice was hard and unforgiving. That he was bothered by her being with another man encouraged her. Their relationship—and she used that word loosely—consisted of surreptitious meetings at his place to fuck. Sure, they talked and laughed and shared intimate moments together that didn't involve the exchange of bodily fluids. He'd even let her spend the night once, but she wanted more.

She'd had a thing for Mark the minute she laid eyes on him. He was gorgeous. Dark blond hair, often unruly on his head. Deep green eyes that made her sigh every single time he looked her direction. Standing at five feet, nine inches barefoot, Suzie struggled to find a guy that made her feel feminine. Mark did. He was tall, over six feet by several inches, and his clothes did nothing to disguise his muscular physique underneath.

But it had been more than his looks. He'd always treated her with respect, even through his own relentless flirting. She didn't make her feelings known right away because he had been married and she wasn't *that* kind of girl. After his divorce, he didn't seem interested in anything more than a one-night-stand and she couldn't risk her heart on that despite her attraction to him. Yet, now here she was, risking her heart for just a little piece of his time, a piece of him.

She pressed herself against his hard body. Her hands sculpted the muscular planes of his back through his light grey dress shirt.

"I don't want another man's hands on me," she said. She glided her hands up over his shoulders and around his neck, interlocking her fingers together. "Just yours."

"Really?" His gaze bore into her. "Is that why I just pulled you out from between two men who were groping you?" Though his gaze was unyielding, she noticed the softness behind his eyes. Underneath the tough "I-don't-want-a-relationship" exterior was a man that wanted a relationship.

"I'm sorry," she said. Her hands caressed the back of his neck as her hips swayed back and forth, brushing against his pelvis. His erection bulged against her belly and excitement coursed through her. She loved his body's reaction to her.

They'd been fooling around for several weeks now and every time she showed up at his place, he took her immediately. Against the front door. Bent over the couch. On the kitchen counter. She'd barely set her purse down and he was on her like white on rice. She loved it. None of her past relationships had even a quarter of the passion.

"We shouldn't be seen together like this," he said. Her heart sunk just a bit at his words. She knew his position on the board was an issue for him, but it still didn't ease the pang in her chest when he made it seem like it was impossible for them to even have a chance. John Dorsey, one of his buddies on the board, had an open relationship with one of Advantage's corporate in-house counsel, Elizabeth Wright. So, why couldn't the two of them have a shot?

Suzie turned around in his arms, placing her back to his chest and bringing his hands to her hips. Rotating her pelvis, her behind worked against his straining erection.

His fingers tangled in her hair and pulled it off her neck. His breath hit just behind her ear, heating her skin. Her body shuddered at his hard pants.

"You trying to make me come in my pants?" he asked. His voice was rough. The fingers on his other hand dug into her hip, pulling her back even harder against him.

"Do you want to come?" Tilting her head to the side, the feral look in his eyes was all the answer she needed.

"I don't want to come in my pants," he said sharply. "But if you keep rubbing your sweet little ass all over me, I may not have a choice." His head fell to her neck and his breath tickled her skin. When his lips brushed just behind her ear, a moan escaped her. His tongue flicked out at that spot just below her ear, causing her body to tremble. What he could do with that tongue!

"You have choices," she said, almost breathless, rotating her hips slowly against him. "You can come in me."

"Fuck," he growled at her words. His hands gripped her hips and pushed her away. Turning to look at him, the turmoil on his face pained her. She wanted to ease his discomfort.

"Mark." Her hand reached for his shirt, but he grabbed her wrist and held it.

Taking a step toward her, he whispered, "You're killing me, baby." His grip on her wrist tightened. "I'm seconds away from lifting your skirt and taking you right here on the dance floor. I'm hard as a rock." Releasing her wrist, he spun on his heels and headed for the small, dark hallway she imagined held the restrooms. She rubbed her wrist that tingled from his grip just seconds before. She wanted this man more than she wanted anything else in her life. She'd do just about anything to make him happy—to make him hers.

"Fuck it." She stalked after him. He slipped behind the black door marked "Men," and she followed suit before it closed all the way, locking the door behind her. The bathroom was dark, lit by a dim recessed light above the sink. The brown stone tiled walls gave the room an elegant sort of feel, much like the rest of the club.

"What the hell are you doing?" he asked, turning to see her standing with her back pressed against the door. The hunger in his eyes almost took her breath away.

"What are *you* doing?" Her gaze raked over him, taking in the contours of his fully clothed frame. His broad chest stretched his grey shirt, making her fingers twitch to unbutton it and expose that wall of muscle that he worked so hard for. He stood with his backside against the sink, gripping the edge of the counter with his hands.

"Baby, I'm so hard right now, I ache. You've brought me to the brink with little effort. I needed a few minutes to calm down. Apparently, you don't want to give me that." His voice cracked with edginess. His restraint waned and she noticed his knuckles turning white from the strength of his grip on the counter.

Taking three steps forward, she set her Pursecase on the counter before reaching her hand out and cupping his erection through his pants. He moaned and his head fell back.

"I want to calm you down," she whispered. She pressed her lips against his neck, flicking her tongue out to taste the salty, masculine flavor of his skin. When his head came forward and his eyes opened, she inhaled deeply at the sight of him. His eyes were the deepest green she'd ever seen them and his lips quirked into a devilish grin. She'd pushed him and he'd reached his limit.

"On your knees, baby," he growled. Excitement coursed through her, heating her from head to toe. Arousal pooled in her low belly and between her legs, soaking her panties. She loved when he turned all domineering alpha male on her. "The only thing that is going to calm me down is your mouth wrapped around my cock." She whimpered at his words as she sank to her knees on the floor of the restroom. The tile was cold and hard against her knees, but she didn't care. A soak in a hot bath would cure the aches and pains later. Right now, he was hers.

Her fingers fumbled with the button and zipper of his pants, wanting desperately to free his beautiful cock. He assisted in opening his pants and pushing his black boxer briefs down just enough to expose his erection. His cock, heavy and hard, bobbed in front of her. The silky skin pulled tight, making his thick veins prominent.

Leaning forward, her tongue laved the length of him from root to tip before engulfing the head of his cock in her mouth.

"Fuck," he cried. His hands grasped the back of her head. "Look at me, baby. Look. At. Me. I want to see your eyes while you fuck me with that amazing mouth of yours."

He was a dirty talker during sex and Suzie loved it. Loved. It. Few things turned her on more than Mark's sexy voice commanding her. Turning her eyes up to his, the lust in his gaze made her lose control. Gripping the base of his cock with her hand, she worked her mouth up and down his length, all the while his hips pumped into her.

Chapter Three

"Oh God! That's it!"

Mark looked down the length of his still clothed body to the blonde beauty staring up at him. Her crystal blue eyes gleamed with desire as her pink tongue flicked out over the engorged head of his rock hard cock before engulfing it with her mouth again. His hand tangled in her blonde mane and palmed the back of her head.

"Deeper, baby," he growled, pulling her head toward him as he pumped his hips forward. His dick hit the back of her throat and it exhilarated him. He'd spent fifteen years married to a woman who, shortly after the honeymoon, refused to suck him off. To find a woman that enjoyed sliding his cock in her mouth and with such vigor as this gorgeous creature made him high. High on adrenaline. High on lust. Few things surpassed a fucking blowjob, even fewer when the blowjob was given by her.

The sucking noises she made as her sweet little mouth pulled on him made him heady. She never once lost eye contact, and the satisfaction in her gaze delighted him. She was with him one hundred percent of the way. Her eyes welled with tears every time he hit the back of her throat, but she never lost eye contact. She intended for him to know that she loved every second of him ramming his cock down her throat, and he loved that she loved it.

"Ahh, fuck," he cried out. His balls tightened and pulled up as the heat coiled in his belly and then shot out to every one of his nerve endings. "Open up, baby," he said, pulling out of her mouth and stroking his length until streams of his cum pulsed onto her tongue and down her throat. He was mesmerized by the constriction of her swallowing as he emptied himself in her mouth. When he had squeezed every last drop of himself out, her lips closed over the head of his cock, her tongue licking him clean.

"Fuck, you're amazing with that mouth," he said harshly, trying to recover from the mind-blowing orgasm. His backside rested against the bathroom countertop as she shimmied up his body and kissed him openly on the mouth. His dick lay flaccid between them, more proof of her keen ability to suck him dry.

"You have an amazing cock," she said sweetly against his lips. "I always knew it would be." She swept her tongue between his lips and into his mouth and he tasted the salty flavor of himself on her tongue. It thrilled him.

To his utter surprise, arousal coursed through his body again with images of bending her over the bathroom counter and fucking her senseless in front of the large mirror. He had to have her. His tongue penetrated her mouth and danced with her tongue. She moaned into him, pressing her tight form even more into him.

Her slim model-like body had turned him on from the moment he had laid eyes on her years ago. Without heels, she stood just five inches shy of his six-foot-three frame. With heels tonight, they were almost eye to eye.

His hand weaved into her long blonde hair and held her lips to his as he kissed her thoroughly.

Mark's other hand toyed with the hem of her dress and his knuckles caressed the soft skin of her thighs. She sighed into his mouth and he took that as affirmation for him to continue. Inching up her inner thigh, the tempo of her breathing increased and her legs separated slightly. The heat from her core warmed his hand the closer he moved to her center.

"Fuck, baby, you're soaked," he growled against her mouth, his fingers touching her already moist panties.

Pulling her panties aside, he made contact with the slick flesh of her pussy. Breaking their kiss, her head fell back as she mewled, closing her eyes. Mark slid his fingers through her smooth folds, collecting all her juices from her center and bringing them forward as he swirled his finger over and around her clit.

"Mark," she moaned. Her body slumped against his, her hands gripping his biceps for support. Slipping his hand free from the back of her head, he grasped her hip, holding her upright while he continued to assault that little bundle of nerves that would push her over the edge.

"That's it, baby. Come for me." He watched her facial features contort in ecstasy. Slipping a finger to her opening, he hovered over it, teasing her body's entrance.

"I need you," she begged, hiking her leg over his hip, resting her foot on the counter's edge, and giving him better access to her pussy. Her cream leaked on to his fingers and coated his hand, the scent of which wafted to his nostrils and made him eager to taste her.

"What do you need?" He licked and sucked the long column of her neck, paying particular attention to the little area that vibrated with her pulse.

"I need you inside me," she pleaded.

"Like this?" he asked, slipping his middle finger inside her hot channel. Her pussy clamped down on his finger as it intruded her body. His thumb circled her clit, then pressed on it, and her body quivered.

"More." Her hips undulated against his hand. He smiled against her neck as he slipped a second finger inside her. Fuck! She was tight! Always tight! The thought of filling her tightness with his cock made his erection thicken.

"How's that, baby?" He penetrated her cunt with two fingers, all the while watching her body react to his ministrations. Her head hung back, cascading her straight blonde hair down her back. Her eyelashes caressed her flushed cheeks, her tiny nostrils flared, and her lips separated with each breath she took. Her fingers dug into his biceps, almost to the point of pain, but he didn't care.

He'd fantasized a number of times over the years of knowing her what it would be like to bring her to the precipice of an orgasm and then fling her over it. Now that he knew what that was like, he had a hard time keeping himself from doing it all the time. Here he was, finger fucking her in the men's restroom at his favorite hangout.

No one had to know about this rendezvous in the restroom of the Beach Club or the multitude of times they met at his place. His seat on the board of directors and her job at Advantage would be safe, but he needed this…needed her in this moment.

"Oh God, Mark," she whimpered. "I'm going to come." Her body twitched and her pussy clenched down on his fingers just before she screamed out his name. Her standing leg gave out and Mark gripped her waist tightly with one arm while his thumb stroked over her clit, drawing out the last tremors from her orgasm.

"That was beautiful," he whispered in her ear. Suzie's leg lowered from the counter and her body slumped forward into him. Pulling his fingers free from her body, he wrapped his arms around her and held her tight. He'd never admit it out loud, but he enjoyed their intimate moments after they exhausted each other.

"I want you to fuck me," she said, raising her head from his shoulder and looking him in the eyes. Her eyes dilated to the point that only slivers of blue were visible. Her hips pushed forward against his erection and he groaned in pleasure. His cock, having not been stuffed back into his pants before he got her off, strained between their bodies.

"Come on," yelled a male from the other side of the locked door. That person banged on the door.

Damn it! How long had they been in there? And how many people would see them walk out of the men's restroom together?

"Shit," Mark said. Grasping her shoulders, he pushed her back a little. The corners of her mouth slid down in disappointment.

While he'd love nothing more than to bend her over the counter and stuff his cock inside her tight warmth, they were in the restroom of a local beach bar on a Saturday night. Plenty of people knew him. Some may even know Suzie. He tucked his dick back into his pants and straightened out his shirt.

"I'd love nothing more than to bury myself inside your hot little cunt right now, baby, but we can't risk this. They'll have one of the security guys break down this door soon if we don't get out of here, and they'd catch us in quite a compromising position."

"Very true. Those security guards are nothing to mess with." She winked at him, even though the smile she plastered to her face didn't reach her eyes. She smoothed out the black shift dress and finger-combed her tangled hair. "Damn it! My mascara ran."

She wet a paper towel and dabbed at the black smudges underneath her eyes before tossing the towel in the trash. She slipped her Pursecase with her iPhone over her wrist and looked at herself in the mirror.

"Do you have a ride home?" Mark stared at her reflection in the mirror. The remaining sparkle in her eyes disappeared at his question and he realized she'd hoped to go home with him. Sure, he wanted to take her home and finish what they had started, but his brain interfered with his desires, with his heart.

Fuck! Did I just say "heart?" Man, I'm royally fucked.

"My friend Lisa is here. We drove together," Suzie said. Her voice was soft.

"Did you fall in the toilet in there?" the man on the other side of the door said, pounding on it again. "I'm going to get security."

"On the way, dude," Mark said, impatience evident in his voice.

"Alright, I'll go first." She walked toward the door. He admired the magnificent way she put herself back together after performing a spectacular blowjob and being finger-fucked to orgasm. She was the kind of woman that allowed him to live out all his fantasies. She was hot. Hotter than he had ever imagined and he feared he was going to ruin her. Or was it that she was going to ruin him and his "stay single" plan?

Suzie unlocked the restroom door and turned to look at him one last time before she sauntered out into the club's darkened hallway. The sadness in her eyes caused an ache in his chest, but he didn't have much time to dwell on it because he heard the hoots and hollers as she exited the restroom. His skin crawled and his vision blurred with red at the idea that any of those guys standing out there envisioned themselves with her. Not to mention, he was pissed at himself for not going with her and protecting her from the walk of shame.

"Mark Olson! Should have figured," said a snarky male voice Mark recognized. He turned from the mirror to see Seth Kriken standing in the small restroom with him. Seth managed one of the competing car dealerships in the St. Petersburg area and knew how to get under Mark's skin. He'd been crawling under it since high school.

Seth and Mark's parents had been friends and attempted on many occasions to force a friendship between the boys, but Seth hadn't wanted to be friends with Mark. He wanted to be better than Mark. That made a friendship impossible. Mark had been outdoing Seth since high school in sports, grades, and girls, and it really stuck in Seth's craw.

Best known for his cheesy car salesman commercials, Seth personally starred in each and every one. He'd jump around shouting at the screen about how low his prices were. In more than one commercial, he made implications as to the quality of cars his competitors sold, mainly meaning Mark's dealerships. Mark had spent hours with his attorneys trying to put a stop to Seth's slanderous ads. He knew Seth's jealousy went deeper than just Mark's successful business.

No love was lost between them.

"Seth," Mark said dispassionately.

"Did that blonde bombshell blow you in here?" Seth asked, running his stubby fingers through his short red hair.

"Wouldn't you like to know." Mark laughed before scooting past Seth and grabbing the door handle to exit the restroom. He had no intention of having this conversation, or any other for that matter, with Seth.

Seeing the red exit sign, Mark walked down the short hallway and pushed through the door, out into the humid salty Florida July air. Taking a deep breath, he leaned against the outside wall of the club, listening to the waves crash against the shore.

Damn it all to hell!

Suzie turned him on, always had, but how could he be so reckless? It wasn't just his seat on Advantage's board of directors that worried him. If Seth found out Suzie's position at Advantage, he'd make it into some sort of scandal, not caring if he took Suzie down with Mark. His stomach churned with acid and the remnants of his whiskey at the thought of hurting her any more than he already had.

Shit! What now?

Chapter Four

"Suzie," her girlfriend, Lisa Elliott, called as Suzie rounded the corner from the hallway to the main area of the club. Suzie's heart sat in her gut after it became clear Mark wasn't going to ask her back to his place. She'd just given one of the best blowjobs of her life and he dismissed her. Sure, he brought her some pleasure, but it took everything she had to keep the tears from welling in her eyes. She couldn't let Mark, or anyone else for that matter, see her break down. Maybe there really was no chance for anything more than sex with Mark.

Could she accept that? The question weighed heavy on her heart.

Suzie forced a smile at her friend, who sat by herself at the bar nursing a glass of red wine. Neither of them had ever been to the Beach Club. They usually hung out downtown St. Petersburg at the eclectic Push Ultra Lounge or the Pour House drinking beers or wine with friends. Those places were open, lively, and young.

The Beach Club was a bit different. Dark wood paneled the walls and bar. The wooden high-top tables around the bar were dark with four black leather chairs encompassing each. The lighting was dim as if in an attempt to hide all its patrons' little secrets. If it weren't for the large window behind the bar that opened to the outside patio area and the sound of the Gulf of Mexico, the place could be mistaken for a swank club as opposed to a beachy one.

Most of the women that gathered at the club appeared to be looking for sugar daddies or just a good time. Dressed in less clothes than lingerie models, they sauntered and shimmied around the men, who flashed their Rolex watches and their glasses filled with Johnnie Walker Blue. And the men...ha! Except for Mark, none of them appeared to own a personality. They had a certain expectation of what the ladies wanted—money! It would be easy to make nothing more than a physical connection here, and that was exactly why Mark loved this place.

She'd overheard him talking to his buddies on the board about his wild nights out at the Beach Club. For almost three years, she'd listened to him rant and rave about all the *pussy* he "tapped." Shaking her head, she realized perhaps Mark didn't want anything more than just a good time from her.

"How'd the dance go with Prince Charming?" Suzie asked her friend. Lisa's long, sandy brown hair twisted and twirled in waves down her back as she ran her finger around the rim of her glass of wine. When Suzie escaped to the restroom after Mark, Lisa had been dancing with a forty-something guy on the dance floor.

"He's no Prince Charming," Lisa laughed, rolling her hazel eyes at Suzie. "More like Prince Charmless." Suzie laughed back. She and Lisa had been good friends since college. Having both graduated from the University of South Florida in Tampa, they moved to St. Pete together for their jobs. Lisa spent the last several years as an accounting associate at a small local firm. Suzie spent her time since college working her way up the ranks to being the executive assistant to Advantage Insurance Company's CEO. She had a knack for organizing and running an office.

She loved her job. Michael treated her well. The company treated her well. In fact, most things in her life were going well, except for her love life. After dating several frogs, Suzie decided to focus her attention on the other aspects of her life, like her career, her friends, and family. Before she knew it, she turned thirty and had no man to share her life.

Now all she wanted was Mark.

From the moment she met him, something sparked inside of her. Initially, she backed off him after his divorce and directed her attention to the two other single men on the board of directors, John Dorsey and Greg Snow. Both of those gentlemen appeared to have their heads on straight and hadn't recently gone through a messy a divorce. But deep down, Mark held her interest. Just a mere smile in her direction caused her heart to race and arousal to pump through her at full force.

After John and Greg found themselves women, Suzie knew she had to do what her heart told her to do…go after Mark Olson. So she did. The sex was amazing. *Amazing*. But it didn't appear to be going anywhere further than that at this point.

"Where'd you go?" Lisa sipped on her glass of red wine. Suzie sat on the bar stool next to her friend and watched the people socializing on the outdoor patio. Her friend eyed her thoroughly before breaking out into a smile.

"What?" Suzie asked, avoiding eye contact with her best friend.

"Did you do him in the parking lot?" Lisa asked. "I know you've been after this Mark guy for some time and you guys have been meeting up."

"I didn't *do him* in the parking lot." Suzie tried to sound appalled. Her behavior with Mark tonight had been completely out of character. Suzie didn't follow guys into the men's restroom to give them a blowjob. In fact, she'd never done that before in her life, but for some reason, Mark compelled her to expose herself to him in ways she never had. She never thought she'd enjoy getting her ass spanked either, but every time Mark's hand slapped down on her bare ass, she came like a freight train.

Perhaps tonight had been a mistake. Coming here to his hangout without any warning may have ruined any shot at convincing him to give them a chance. Maybe he was pissed.

What does he think of me now?

Glancing around the club, she didn't see Mark anywhere. It was as if he never left the restroom. Her heart sunk. He snuck out without even facing her and that stung.

"Then where the hell were you for the last twenty minutes or so, because I sure as fuck didn't see you on the dance floor?"

"Don't worry about it," Suzie said with a forced smile.

"Hey there," a man said, approaching them from behind at the bar.

Glancing over her shoulder, Suzie thought he looked familiar. Wiry red hair curled on the top of his head and his hazel eyes studied her closely. Too closely. But she couldn't place him. He wasn't the kind of guy that would reap a second look from her if she passed him on the street, so she couldn't figure out where she knew him. She gripped Lisa's arm tightly, not liking the feeling the situation garnered.

"What is it?" Suzie asked, turning around on her stool to face the stranger.

"Aren't you the babe that hooked up with Mark Olson in the restroom tonight?" The redhead's gaze roamed over her body and a chill rumbled through Suzie.

Shit! He must have been the guy banging on the door.

Suzie had walked out of the restroom, head held high, and simply ignored the few people that had gathered in the hallway. They didn't know she hadn't just gone in the men's room to use it because the women's restroom had been occupied.

"Hey," Lisa said, swiveling around to face the man too. Her eyes narrowed at him, showing her protectiveness of Suzie. "I don't know what you're talking about, but I suggest you take it elsewhere." The redhead glanced over at Lisa before dismissing her with a huff and a hand wave.

"Come on, babe," he continued, taking a few steps closer to Suzie. His arms crossed over his chest, emphasizing his bulky bicep muscles, but he appeared to be top-heavy. His black slacks clung to his hips by a belt. "I saw you walk out of that restroom, and Mark was in there when I went in. I'd treat you better than Olson, sweetheart. He left the building immediately after your *hook up*. He's an ass like that. I see it happen every weekend. He walks out of here with a different girl every weekend. Sometimes more than one. Why don't you let me buy you a drink and make everything all right?"

"I'm sorry," Suzie said. She attempted to disguise the hurt that bubbled up inside of her at the idea that Mark had just up and left without saying anything to her.

Christ! I am such a fucking idiot!

She'd have to see him next week for the third quarter board meeting. How awkward was that going to be? "I don't know what you're talking about, nor do I know who you are."

"I'm Seth Kriken," he said, holding out his hand to her. Suzie looked at his hand and then stood up. She towered over him by at least eight inches with her heels.

"Good to know," she said, ignoring Seth's outstretched hand and grabbing Lisa's arm. Yanking Lisa from her stool, she pulled her friend in the direction of the front door, never glancing back to look at Seth. "Let's get out of here."

"Fine with me," Lisa replied. "I haven't seen any worthy prospects all night."

Seth Kriken! Seth Kriken! Now she knew where she recognized him. Seth ran a car dealership—Kriken Kars—in St. Petersburg. His face was plastered over multiple billboards around Pinellas County and his commercials played regularly on the TV. He was Mark's direct competition and nemesis. *Oh crap!*

"So, are you going to tell me what the hell is going on?" Lisa asked as they climbed into Suzie's white Toyota Camry.

"Nothing's going on." Suzie started the car and pulled out of the Beach Club parking lot, heading in the direction of hers and Lisa's condo downtown.

"Suzie, you're talking to me," Lisa reassured her. "That short little creep was not just hitting on you, but was degrading the man you've been after for quite some time. What was he talking about the restroom?"

"I followed Mark into the men's restroom and locked the door," Suzie said emphatically. She felt Lisa's gaze on her. "What?" She turned to her friend, who sat silent beside her.

"You did him in the men's restroom of a packed club?" Lisa asked, the shock thick in her voice.

"We didn't do *it*," Suzie said, drawing her attention back to the road.

"What the hell did you do? And why was that Seth guy coming after you?" Lisa said, concern evident in her voice.

"We fooled around," Suzie explained. "And I don't know why Seth was sniffing around other than I know he's Mark's main competitor in the area. They own competing car dealerships. I think he's always trying to one-up Mark. Mark doesn't talk about him other than to say that it isn't a friendly competition. You know…that whole Napoléon complex." Lisa laughed, which in turn, caused Suzie to laugh.

"Fooling around in the men's restroom at a club," Lisa said. "Tsk. Tsk. I never thought I'd see the day."

Suzie could hear the smile and pride in her friend's voice. Lisa was always trying to get her to loosen up, let her hair down. Not that her friend encouraged her to sleep around, but Lisa knew she had a thing for Mark. Suzie waved her hand in the direction of Lisa like she was shooing away a fly, but she couldn't help the slight smile that spread across her face.

The guys she'd dated over the years never sparked her in the bedroom. She'd been physically attracted to them…initially, but no one lit her up like a firecracker the way Mark did. He made her want to try new things, to test her boundaries. The few weeks they'd been sneaking around had been the most exciting weeks of sex she'd ever had. The intimate moments they'd shared afterwards had been filled with feelings…true feelings. She knew there was something between them. How could she make him see they were good together?

"You might want to warn your lover boy about this Seth guy," Lisa warned.

Suzie pulled the car into the driveway of their parking deck and rolled down the driver's side window. She slid her parking pass in front of the scanner and waited until the bar rose before driving inside.

"Why? Do you think he's up to something?" Suzie's mind reeled at what Seth's agenda could possibly be.

"You said he may be trying to one-up Mark. He came at you shortly after you returned from the restroom. Maybe he had a confrontation with Mark beforehand. I'm

133

just saying I'd give him a heads up about this Seth guy." Suzie parked her Toyota in her designated spot and killed the engine.

"I'll text him right now." She flipped her pink Pursecase over and pressed the button on her iPhone. Swiping her finger across and tapping in her passcode, she scrolled for Mark's cell phone.

"Seth Kriken cornered me at club. Said some nasty stuff about u and tried to buy me drink. Seemed to b up to something."

She pressed send on her phone and climbed out of the car. Lisa stood next to the trunk waiting on her.

"I'm beat. All that flirting exhausted me," Lisa said. "Those rich men out on the beach are high maintenance. No thanks."

Both girls chuckled as they walked to the door of their building. Lisa swiped her keycard and the buzzer sounded. They walked into the large atrium toward the elevator that would take them to their sixth floor condo. Lisa pressed the call button and the doors immediately opened, both girls stepping inside the small elevator. As the doors slid closed, Suzie's phone chimed. Flipping her Pursecase over, Mark's text lit up her screen.

"Fuck him. Please tell me u didn't let him buy u a drink. R u on ur way home?"

The fact that he responded to her text after the way he left the club was enough to make her smile, but that he didn't want her even taking a drink from this Seth guy elated her for some reason.

"I don't want to fuck him. I want to fuck u. No drink. In the elevator. On my way up to my condo."

Suzie lifted her head to see Lisa staring at her with a knowing look.

"What?" Suzie asked, trying to keep her smile contained.

"Are you sexting him now?" Lisa teased as Suzie's phone chimed again.

"Thanks for not taking the drink. He's an asshole. Glad u made it home safely. And baby, I love fucking you."

What the hell? How did she respond to that? He loved fucking her. Okay! Then why did he bolt from the club without a word to her? Why didn't he offer to take her home? Her head jumbled with all sorts of questions she wanted to ask him when the elevator dinged for their floor. The doors slid open and both Suzie and Lisa's mouths dropped open when they saw Mark. He stood in the hallway with his back against the wall, his hands stuffed in his pants pockets and a sheepish smile on his lips. Suzie's heart pounded against her ribs.

Chapter Five

Yep, Mark had been an asshole. If he could, he would have kicked his own ass for leaving the Beach Club without saying a word to Suzie. The last thing he wanted to do was make her feel like she was cheap or that he didn't respect her. He knew his swift departure left her reeling and that had made his chest constrict so tight that it scared him shitless.

Hightailing it across town, he had persuaded a resident of her building to buzz him in. He made a mental note to talk to her about the safety of her building. Living downtown St. Petersburg was typically safe, but it didn't sit right with him that the residents would buzz any Joe Schmoe into the building. Scanning the mailboxes, he had recognized her last name and rode the elevator to the sixth floor to wait.

The wait had felt like forever. Scenarios played out in his head. Maybe she and her friend hit another club or bar. Maybe neither was capable of driving. That worried him. He hadn't known exactly how much she'd had to drink, but she had been brazen in her actions with him. He didn't want her driving intoxicated. Maybe she went home with someone else. That last scenario made his stomach churn and his jaw clench. He didn't like that idea at all. Despite all his denial and rationale, he wanted her for himself.

When he received her text message while standing in her building hallway, his anger kicked up a notch at the idea that Seth would make a play for her. That man would do anything to get under his skin. Guilt at leaving her there to deal with Seth's underhanded behavior rolled through him. But when she indicated she was on her way up to her condo, relief set in. He just needed to see her. When those doors slid open, his breath caught at the sight of her.

"Mark," Suzie exclaimed. Her back pressed against the rear wall of the elevator, her blue eyes widened in surprise. Her long tendrils cascaded over her shoulder and her mouth was agape. She clutched her phone to her chest. Her friend, Lisa, maintained a similar expression. He couldn't help but chuckle.

"Are you going to get out of the elevator? Or do I need to come in there and get you?" Though his tone was half-teasing, there was a serious element to his words. He pushed off the wall toward the elevator and placed his hand on the elevator opening to keep the doors from closing.

"I can see why you like him," Lisa said. She turned her head to Suzie in the back of the elevator and smiled before walking out. "Don't break her heart," Lisa whispered as she brushed past him to the door to their condo. "Or I will break your face." Mark immediately liked Lisa because it was clear she was a good friend to Suzie.

"What are you doing here? How'd you get in the building?" Suzie hadn't moved from her spot in the rear of the elevator.

"I'm here because I owe you an apology. Because I wanted to see you. We'll talk about how I got in here and why you need to talk to the association about security later." Striding into the elevator, he placed a hand next to either side of her head, caging her against the wall. His head lowered and he pressed his lips gently to hers.

"Mark." She gasped against his lips. Pulling back from the kiss, he ran his thumb over her bottom lip.

"I'm so sorry I left you there," he said. His gaze met hers and his heart constricted when he noticed her watery eyes. "It was a selfish and shitty thing to do and I don't blame you if you hate me or never want to see me again. I've been so concerned about what others would think if they saw us together. That being together could ruin my seat on the board. I completely disregarded your feelings. You deserve so much better than me." Her eyes closed and a lone tear escaped down her cheek. He brushed it away with his thumb and his chest tightened.

"I don't want anyone else," she said. Her voice was so soft he almost couldn't hear her.

"I don't want you to want anyone else," he said. His heart beat rapidly. Just the idea of her giving herself to somebody else had his knees weaken. "I'm so, so sorry."

"It's okay," she whispered. She opened her eyes and met his gaze. Emotion fluttered in their blue depths.

"It's not okay."

"I'm fine." She lowered her gaze to the floor. "You must think I'm a real slut after my behavior earlier."

With his thumb and forefinger under her chin, he tilted her head to meet his stare. "Baby, I'd never think that about you. Ever. I love the fact that you aren't afraid to show your sexual side, that you are open to new ideas and experiences. That you're spontaneous." He lowered his lips to hers again, the pressure hard in his kiss. His tongue swept out at the seam of her lips and she gasped. Her reaction allowed him to slip his tongue between her lips to tangle with her own, exploring.

He needed to settle down or he'd be taking her against the elevator wall. Not that that idea didn't have appeal, but she deserved more than just a quick fuck tonight. She deserved to be cherished. Loved.

Pulling back from the kiss, he released a sharp exhale and stared at her again. "I realize it's my actions, my leaving you at that club, that caused you to think that, and I am so sorry. I never want you to feel that way, especially because of something I do or say."

The elevator doors slid closed behind them and he reached to the front to press the Open button. The doors skated open again. He needed to lighten the mood. He had hurt her and he realized his wrongdoing. He'd spent the last three years dilly-dallying around with a bunch of women that brought him nothing more than an orgasm. This woman—*this* woman made his heart beat faster. Whatever the cost, she was worth it.

Damn! It took you long enough, Olson.

Picking her up by the waist, he tossed her over his shoulder. Her yelp made him grin. His arm clutched her smooth legs tightly to keep her in position. Her torso squirmed down his back as he walked in the direction of the door Lisa disappeared behind. God, he hope she left the door unlocked.

"Where are you taking me?" She bit over his shirt into the hard flesh of his low back just above his buttocks. The pinch from her little bite sent a jolt through his limbs and gave him and instant hard-on. He enjoyed a little pain with his pleasure and she knew that. She also knew he loved nothing more than her submission.

"A little feisty, eh?" he said, pushing through her front door. Their small condo immediately felt like walking into a Pottery Barn catalogue. The caramel couch by the far wall was adorned with wine-colored pillows. A leather rectangular ottoman with a wicker tray stacked with books and a large wooden and bronze lantern perched in front of the cushiony couch. The beige carpet was plush and the walls were decorated with frame after frame of the girls and their friends and family. It was definitely an invitingly warm home.

Lisa stood in their kitchen by the sink with a glass of water in her hand and a smile stretched on her face.

"Second door on the left," Lisa said, jerking her head in the direction of the hallway.

Mark winked at her before traipsing down the hall to Suzie's bedroom. Opening the door, he was taken aback by her bedroom. He'd envisioned her as a girly-girl, decorated in bright pinks or yellows with flowers or butterflies.

Instead, he was greeted by a simply elegant bedroom. Slate-colored walls bordered an off-white dresser and four-poster bed. A lavender duvet comforter covered the queen-sized mattress with two silver throw pillows askew. Scrawled in black script on a white canvas hung above her bed was the quote, "When you love what you have, you have everything you need." His lips pulled at the corners. Not only did she wear her heart on her sleeve, she decorated her room with it.

Striding over to her lush bed, he tossed her on it. Her body bounced gently and a giggle escaped her. God, he loved that sound. Happiness.

"What are you doing?" she asked between giggles. Her blonde hair spread out around her head like a halo. Her black dress rode up her legs, revealing more of her creamy thighs than he could handle. Wrapping his hands around her ankles, he pulled her to the edge of the bed.

"I'm going to take your shoes off." He rested her ankles on his shoulders. Brushing his lips softly along the inside of her ankle, his adept fingers unbuckled the clasp on one high-heeled sandal than the other before slipping them off her feet and letting them fall to the floor. "I'm going to remove these panties." His hands smoothed down the inside of her thigh and her breath caught as he inched closer to her core. Looping his fingers around the sides of her panties, he slid them down her legs and over her feet. Bringing her panties to his nose, he inhaled deeply. "Damn! I love the way you smell."

Dropping to his knees next to the bed, he set her feet on his shoulders and spread her legs wide. Her pussy lips, dusted lightly with short blonde hair, were plump and wet with desire. His mouth watered for a taste. Her musky feminine scent enveloped him until he was lightheaded. Leaning forward, he lapped the seam of her pussy, drawing all her juices on his tongue.

"I love the way you taste even more," he said. Working her center with his tongue, her hips writhed against his mouth as she tried to coax him where she wanted him. Pinning her thighs open with his forearms, he licked, suckled, and ate at her core like he was a starving man. Her sweet flavor burst on his tongue with each swipe, but he purposely stayed away from the little bundle of nerves that he knew would cause her to explode.

"Mark," she whimpered. Her hands tangled in his hair, trying desperately to position his mouth on her clit. Raising his gaze to look at her from his position between her legs, her eyes pled with him.

"What is it, baby? What do you want?" he asked before spearing her opening with his tongue.

"Oh God!" Her breathing was hard, her chest rising and falling in rapid succession. Having had sex with her multiple times over the last several weeks, he knew she was close. Her fingers pulled and tugged at his hair. The muscles in her legs tightened under his restraint. "Please!"

"Please what?" He nipped at her outer lips before slipping a finger inside of her.

"Please make me come!" she cried. Her body tensed at the invasion.

Pumping his finger in and out of her pussy, his mouth covered that bundle of nerves that stood hard and ready, begging for him to unleash on it. His tongue lashed it, once, twice, before he pulled it into his mouth and sucked on it. His gaze stayed glued to her face. Squeezing her eyes shut, she bit into her lower lip as she came undone under him. Her walls clenched around his finger, and her hips bucked as her fingers tangled in his hair, holding his face against her. Shuddering, she released all the tension she'd been holding in her muscles as she cascaded over the cliff into ecstasy.

A realization hit him hard as he watched her come down from her pleasure. He wanted to own her. Possess her. God damn it all to hell…he wanted to love her.

Chapter Six

Coming down from that orgasm wasn't easy. Stars flickered behind Suzie's eyes and her entire body floated in an ethereal state. It was surreal where he could bring her.

After Mark had brushed her off at the club, she expected to come home and sulk, throw herself a pity party. Maybe share a pint of chocolate chip cookie dough ice cream with Lisa and watch *The Notebook*. But this, *this* was incredible.

Rising from his position on the floor, Mark stood at the edge of bed, arms crossed over his broad chest, standing between her legs, looking like a man that just conquered the world. His dark blond hair sat ruffled and unkempt on his head, no doubt from her fingers pulling him into her. His eyes sparkled a darker shade of green, demonstrating his level of desire. Sweeping his tongue out over his plump lower lip, he tasted the remnants of her juices on his glistening lips and moaned.

"Fuck! You're amazing," he said, working his fingers over the buttons on his shirt. Once his shirt was completely unbuttoned, he pushed it down his arms and flung it to the floor. "Now, I'm going to make love to you." Pulling a strand of condoms from his pants pocket, he threw them on the bed.

"That's a lot of condoms," she said. Her voice was breathy and taunting.

"There's a lot of love to be made, baby." His mouth turned up on one side before he started shedding his pants.

Suzie propped herself up on her elbows as she watched him remove the rest of his clothes. Her gaze roamed over him from head to toe. His body was fantastic. If she didn't know he was forty-one years old, she'd never guess it. Broad solid shoulders flowed down to hard, muscular arms and strong hands that had brought her to the moon and back on more than one occasion. A dash of dark blond hair splattered his defined chest, which led to abs that she could wash her laundry against.

"God, you're beautiful," she blurted. Looking at him standing in front of her naked, she couldn't help but express the way she saw him. All hard, muscular planes of gorgeous male. A small smile stretched his lips. He stalked toward her, looking like a lion on the hunt, and she relished the fact that she was his prey. His.

Climbing on the bed, he grasped the hem of her dress and pulled it smoothly over her head and arms, revealing her black lace bra that did little to hide her rosy, pert nipples. They ached for his attention, straining against the lace. Leaning over her, his mouth closed around one of her nipples as he suckled her through the lace. A guttural moan escaped her. She didn't think it was possible to feel so aroused after the orgasm she just had, but he had a way about him that made her come alive. Lashing her nipple with his tongue, her back arched. Using that opportunity to slip his hands underneath her, he unhooked her bra. Releasing her from his mouth, he sat up on his knees and peeled her bra down her arms.

"Fuck, baby! Beautiful doesn't even begin to describe you. Every time I look at you, it's as exciting as the first time." Covering her body with his own, his mouth found hers, kissing her fiercely. His tongue thrust between her parted lips and licked into her mouth with fervor. Her hands crawled up the length of his strong arms until they circled behind his neck and tangled in his hair, holding him to her as he kissed her like his life depended on it. His cock stood at full attention against her belly, begging to enter her body.

"Make love to me," she whispered against his lips. She nipped at his bottom lip before pulling it into her mouth and sucking on it. A growl rolled through him, vibrating against her chest.

"I know that I hurt your feelings tonight." He pulled back from their kiss, but kept his face close to hers. His hot breath fanned across her face. "I never wanted to hurt you, Suzie. Never. Please know that."

Her eyes softened and tears welled in the corners. "It's okay."

"It's not okay. I acted like a shit. I treated you like you didn't matter to me, and all because I was scared." Resting his forehead against hers, he exhaled slowly. His eyes squeezed shut as if he were struggling to express himself. She wanted to save him.

"You're here now," she whispered. Her hand cupped his cheek, his five o'clock shadow rough against her fingertips.

"I am. I'm here because you do matter to me. A lot. And I have every intention of proving that to you." Nudging her chin forward, she caught his lips with her own and kissed him. Her tongue stroked at his lips and into his mouth, tangling with his tongue. Raising her hips slightly to make contact with his pelvis, she swallowed the growl that ripped from him.

"Show me how you feel, Mark."

Rising to his knees, he grabbed a condom on the bed and tore the package open, tossing the foil to the ground. Her gaze followed his every move, watching his muscles bunch on his chest and biceps as he sheathed his cock. Nudging the head of his cock at her opening, she arched up, ready to accept him.

"Oh God," she cried as the head of his penis breached her opening. Mark wasn't the average lover. He was hung quite well, and it took several moments for her body to accommodate him. Her pussy clung to him, gripping him like a vise as he slid into her inch by slow inch. Demonstrating her impatience, she wrapped her legs around the back of his, cupped his muscular ass in her hands, and pulled him further into her until he was fully seated.

"Ahh! Fuck." His eyes squeezed shut as he inhaled deep. "Every. Time. Baby. You're so damn tight."

"Move, Mark," she whimpered. Her body craved the friction. She needed him to move in her, to rock her into the next dimension with his thrusts. Pulling back until he almost left her body, he drove back into her hard, hitting the very end of her. The noise that left her body from the impact could only be described as primal.

"You like it hard, don't you?" he asked, his gaze finding hers. His dark green eyes were hooded with desire. All she could do was nod in answer to his question. His last several thrusts had quite literally knocked the air out of her lungs and, therefore, her ability to speak as well. Drawing his hips back completely, he left her body and she whimpered in protest. A soft chuckle left him. Gripping her hips, he flipped her on her belly. "Like this. I want to take you like this."

Suzie's heart raced. She loved being taken by him from behind. This was a position that brought the animal out in him and she loved the primitive nature of it. She rose up on her hands and knees, offering her backside to him.

"You have the loveliest ass, baby." His hands caressed her cheeks. The palm of his hand landed on her right cheek, slapping her hard, and she cried out. She knew it was coming, but it always caught her off guard. He soothed the stinging sensation with a soft, gentle stroke of his hand over the area he'd just slapped. "It's even lovelier when it's pink." He smacked her again.

"Ahhh!" Wriggling her hips back toward him, her arousal seeped from her and on to her inner thighs. "I need you inside me."

"Such a greedy little thing," he said. Turning to look over her shoulder, her lips quirked up one side as she smiled at him. "Looking at me like that is only going to get your ass slapped again."

Keeping the sexy grin on her face, she flicked her tongue out over her bottom lip before pulling it between her teeth and thrusting her bottom back against his hips. His hand came down on her other cheek, sending a zinging sensation over her body. Her low back arched as she enjoyed the heat that spread over her.

He grasped her hips with his powerful hands, his fingers digging into her flesh as he positioned her. Reaching under her body, she gripped his cock and guided it to her opening. Driving his hips forward, he impaled her and they both cried out. Holding his hips against her bottom, he filled her completely. In this position, he always went deeper, deeper than any man had ever been. Her head fell forward as she drew in deep breaths. Her lungs burned from the large gasps of oxygen she pulled as her body once again adjusted and relished his invasion of her. He touched her everywhere. His hands moved frantically over her back, around her chest, grasping and massaging her breasts. It was as if he couldn't get enough of her.

"You make me so wild. So goddamn wild." His fingers tangled into her hair and pulled her head back. The spark of discomfort at his pull lasted a whole second before dissipating into a warmth of pleasure. "Look at me, baby. Look at what you do to me." She turned her head to see him. His muscular arms gathered with his hold on her, one hand in her hair, the other gripping her hip. He began to plow into her at full force, his pelvis slamming into her ass, his balls slapping against her clit. His abs rippled with each drive into her. His bottom lip was caught between his teeth. His dark green eyes were filled with unabashed lust, but there was something behind the lust. Something emotional. That's what broke her.

Her body tingled as her impending orgasm reached new heights. Jolts of pleasure shot out to all her nerve endings as her muscles tensed. Her eyes remained trained on Mark as he sought his own release in her body.

"Fuck," he cried, stroking into her fiercely. She exploded. Her pussy contracted around him, milking him, egging on his release as she shuddered around him. "That's it, baby. That's it! Make me come." He growled seconds before he came hard inside her. Watching his eyes squeeze shut as he soared into his orgasm had her sex clenching around him again. He collapsed on top of her, causing her legs and arms to give out as she crumpled to the bed. His chest expanded into her on each deep breath he took.

"You okay?" she asked from underneath him.

Sliding off her back and to her side, he removed the condom, tied it off, and tossed in the trash container next to her bed. Wrapping his arm around her waist, he pulled her into him. "I'm perfect, baby. That was perfect." Snuggling into him, her head resting on his muscular chest, surrounded by his masculine scent, she fell asleep…only to be woken a couple hours later with him between her legs again. He hadn't been lying when he said there was plenty of love to be made.

Chapter Seven

Mark pulled his black Jaguar XK into his St. Petersburg dealership a little after noon and parked in his usual spot by the side door of the showroom. Most weeks he'd cuss out having to run to his dealership during lunch on an Advantage board Friday, but after spending the week with Suzie between her place and his, he couldn't find anything to cuss about. He'd made love to her so many times he thought for sure neither one of them would walk straight for days. Waking up to her this morning all snuggled into him, her eyes closed and her lips parted as she slept so peacefully, he had one thing to do... resign from Advantage's board.

He'd gotten married young and spent fifteen years married to the wrong woman, of that he was sure. He didn't regret it in that it brought him Angela and Laura, his two beautiful daughters, but his marriage had never been a healthy relationship. The claustrophobia that it became ended in a bitter divorce that led to more than three years of philandering with anything that would give him attention. Sometimes, he even disgusted himself.

Now he had the chance to have a meaningful relationship with someone that made him smile and laugh and feel worthy. His role as a member of Advantage's board of directors had been a good one and, in all honesty, it was what led him to Suzie, but he wasn't going to risk her job or their happiness for it.

It took him some soul searching over the past week to realize that leaving his role on the board didn't mean the end of the friendships he'd made, but staying on the board could mean the end of his relationship with Suzie. He'd give Phillip Barker, the chairman of the board, his resignation this afternoon. He finalized that decision in his head as he watched Suzie sleep all snuggled into him this morning.

He'd asked Suzie to put thirty minutes at the end of the board meeting agenda for him to speak to the board. Everyone, including her, had hounded him about the purpose of his reserved time, but he wasn't going to let it slip even though it had almost killed him not to kiss Suzie square on the mouth when he entered the executive suite this morning.

She had sat behind her desk, her hair tied up in a tight bun at the top of her head. A cobalt blue sleeveless sheath dress that brought out the blue of her eyes clung to her frame. When her eyes rose to meet his, his breath caught, making it almost impossible for him to breathe, let alone smile or react to her.

Getting out of his car, he shook his head at the vision of her still stuck in his mind. He had to admit, he lost the battle. He was hopelessly in love with her. Pressing the key fob to lock his car, he walked across the sidewalk and through the all glass showroom of his dealership, waving to a few of the staff members as he made his way to his office in the back corner. He'd pick up the paperwork for his showroom renovation loan and drop it off at the bank before skipping across town to Advantage's offices to wrap up the last part of his last board meeting.

"Mr. Olson," Gloria Hudson said, slamming down the phone. Mark's secretary stood up abruptly from behind her black desk just outside his office. Her dark brown hair was tied back in a ponytail and it swung from side to side from her sudden movement.

"Morning, Gloria," he said, smiling at her until he noticed her brow was drawn down and the creases in the corners of her eyes as they narrowed. "What's up? You look upset."

Walking over to him, she stopped mere inches in front of him, and her hands started moving in jerky motions as she explained her predicament. "Mr. Kriken is waiting in your office," she whispered. "I told him you would be stopping in for a few minutes to grab some things. I tried to get him to wait out here, but he just brushed past me like he owned the place and made himself at home in your office. I was just about to get Bruce over here to remove him when I saw you walk in. I'm so sorry."

Mark clenched his fists at his sides as irritation and anger coursed through him. He was tired of the constant battle with Seth Kriken. Quite frankly, he was tired of Seth Kriken. Period.

"Thanks, Gloria," he said. His smile sat stiffly on his lips as he walked around her desk to the slightly open door of his office. "Seth," he said, swinging the door open to find the red-headed pain in the ass sitting behind his desk like it was his office. Mark's jaw tightened and his back teeth gnashed together as his anger hiked up a notch.

"Mark! Was wondering when you'd get here," Seth said. A smirk sat on his face, one that Mark would love to wipe off with his fist. Why did this guy cause such a reaction in him? Seth glanced down at his watch and said, "Maybe if you actually worked a bit, you wouldn't have to worry about me or my dealership so much."

Inhaling deeply, Mark stepped into his office and shut the door. No reason for everyone to be subjected to this asshole. Exhaling, he said, "I don't worry about you or your dealership. And please get out from behind my desk before I personally remove you." He crossed his arms over his chest, hoping he appeared as intimidating as he felt in that moment. He'd have no problem grabbing

Seth by his navy blue Kriken Kars polo shirt and literally throwing him off the property, though he was sure that was exactly what Seth was hoping for, some sort of aggression against him in which to exploit Mark.

A sardonic laugh filled the office and the sound grated on Mark's nerves. Amazing how he entered his dealership in a happy mood and now he wanted to rip someone apart...not someone—Seth.

"Aren't you going to even ask why I'm here?"

"I don't really give a shit," Mark said.

"I thought you might want to talk about Suzannah McCormick. I mean, seriously, Olson. Fucking the assistant to Advantage's CEO in a local club bathroom." Seth's head shook from side to side, demonstrating his mock-disapproval.

"Leave Suzie out of this," Mark said through his clenched teeth. He didn't mind if Seth came after him, but it would be a cold day in hell that he'd allow Seth to do anything to Suzie.

"I can't," Seth continued. "You're a tough guy to get an advantage on, but I think if Michael Herron returns my call any time soon, he'll be interested to know that one of his board members is fucking around with his assistant. Who, by the way, does have a sweet voice and ass, but her attitude leaves much to be desired."

Mark dropped his arms to his sides and clenched his fists at Seth's comments about Suzie. The side of his jaw ticked as he gnashed his teeth together.

Seth didn't even pause. "Then there might be questions as to how Advantage is being run and if decisions by the board are really unbiased. I mean, is Michael Herron requesting that his assistant blow you so that you are the deciding vote on key business decisions? Would hate for those pesky local reporters to get a hold of that juicy bit."

"Seth, if you have a problem with me, that's fine. We're both men. Let's handle it."

Seth stood up from behind Mark's desk and placed his stubby hands flat on the desktop. He didn't move from behind the desk as Mark had asked him to do, and Mark suspected it was because he felt a position of power where he was. Attempting to stand face-to-face with Mark would simply emphasize his small stature.

"I like to handle things the way I want to," Seth said. "You and I duking it out doesn't work for me. It's obvious you're bigger than me. Luckily, there are other ways to bring you to your knees." He sneered at Mark.

Grinding his teeth, Mark gripped the back of the small brown leather chair opposite his desk. Blood rushed through his veins and heat rose on his cheeks as his anger built. He inhaled deeply through his nose in an effort to calm himself. "What *is* it you want, Seth?"

"I want to embarrass you. Humiliate you. Make you see what it's felt like all these years being second fiddle to *Mark Olson*."

The way Seth's words seethed with hatred hit Mark like a ton of bricks. In that moment, he realized how miserable Seth really was. All these years, he'd done nothing but agonize over what Mark had and he didn't. Some of the anger and aggression Mark had been feeling moments ago dissipated at this awareness and a feeling close to pity started to fill its spot.

"I'm sorry things have been so rough for you, Seth," Mark said. His voice filled with pity and he didn't attempt to disguise it. "Quite honestly, I hadn't realized you were still so hung up in the past."

"Don't go fucking patronizing me," Seth shouted.

"I'm not. I get the fact that you've been in constant competition with me since high school. High school! At what point do you just grow up and move on,

Seth? But even if you can't get passed your issues, there's no reason you need to drag a good woman or a good company through the mud just to get an edge on me. That's just shitty and childish."

Seth's face flushed red with what Mark recognized as anger. His hands curled into fists on top of Mark's desk and just as he was about to say something, his phone buzzed in the holder strapped to his belt. Pulling out his phone and glancing at the screen, he swiped his fingers across it and said into the phone, "Why hello, Michael. Thanks so much for calling me back." His icy gaze found Mark's. Flipping Mark the middle finger, he opened the office door and sauntered out.

"Fuckity, fuck, fuck," Mark said, slamming his office door shut. He had wanted to be the one to tell Michael about his relationship with Suzie. He didn't want Michael or the rest of the board finding out about it in this way, like he was trying to be underhanded. "God damn it!"

Grabbing the loan documents he'd asked Gloria to put on his desk, he stuffed the folder under his arm and stormed out of his office. He could attempt to chase Seth down, but then what would he do? Beat him to a pulp? He was already on the phone with Michael.

"Mr. Olson?" Gloria asked, looking at him as he rounded her desk. "Is everything okay?"

"Fine, Gloria. Thank you." His voice was stern, sterner than he intended to speak to her. "I'm sorry for snapping at you. I'm headed back to Advantage and will not likely be back in today. Please have Bruce do all the end of day paperwork."

Gloria's lips stretched into a soft but hesitant smile as he turned and headed toward the side door of the showroom. He unlocked his car and slid into its plush leather seats. Starting the engine, he whipped the car out of its parking space and threw it in drive, peeling out with a screech.

He weaved in and out of traffic, zipping down First Avenue South, hoping to avoid most of the traffic lights by taking a one-way road east. Reaching the parking lot next to the Advantage office building, he slammed his car into the first available parking spot and bolted into the building, giving the security guy Sam a quick wave.

If Seth jeopardized Suzie's job, he would kill him. He'd literally kill him. That little prick would stop at nothing to get at Mark and apparently, he'd take down anyone connected to him. Yes, Mark felt pity for him. The guy clearly spent his entire life comparing his to Mark's and had turned out disappointed, but he wasn't going to ruin other people's lives in his seek for revenge.

Taking the stairs two and three at a time, he reached the glass doors of the executive suite in record time. Luckily, he kept himself in shape. Otherwise, he would have been winded.

Scanning his security badge, the door clicked and he rushed in. His mind was set on one thing and that was getting to Michael immediately. Seth had already spilled the beans, but perhaps he could do some damage control as it related to Suzie.

He marched through the reception area of the executive suite. Suzie sat at her desk typing away until she noticed him coming her direction. Her fingers paused over the keyboard as he approached.

"Mark?" Her voice was filled with worry. "What's wrong?"

"I need to see Michael," he said, rounding her desk and heading for the CEO office down the short hallway behind her.

"Mark! Wait," she said, standing. "He's on a phone call." She reached for his arm, but he brushed it away. Her eyes widened at his dismissiveness and she pulled her hand back as if he'd burned her. Hurt settled in her gaze and he paused. He hated seeing that look on her face.

"I'm sorry," he said before hurrying past her and toward Michael's office. The idea of knocking crossed his mind momentarily, but instead, he pushed open the office door to find Michael sitting behind his cherry wood desk, holding the phone receiver to his ear. Michael's eyes enlarged at his entrance, but he waved Mark in and pointed to the chair across the desk opposite him. Mark closed the office door and sat.

"Listen, I've got to go," Michael said. "I appreciate you providing me with this information." Mark couldn't hear what was being said on the other end and his heart beat a little quicker in anticipation. He was sure Seth gave Michael an earful. "I understand completely," Michael said. His voice was short. "We'll handle the situation." Michael slammed the phone down and looked up at Mark. "Well God damn it, Mark. What the hell is going on?"

"I'm sorry this has gotten thrown at your feet, Michael." Mark shifted in the chair and crossed his ankle over his knee. Restless, his fingers combed through his hair.

"Thrown at my feet? That asshole is trying to use your indiscretion with Suzie to destroy more than just you." Michael sat back in his brown leather chair and ran his own hands through his hair, causing it to stand up. "And Suzie? Mark." Michael closed his eyes and shook his head, signifying the disappointment in Mark's actions. "You know she has had a crush on you for quite some time. You can't toy with her. She's a good girl."

"Listen," Mark said. "I had every intention of resigning from the board this afternoon. The time reserved at the end of the schedule today…that was for me to explain all of this to you guys and turn in my resignation."

"Resign? Why?" Michael asked. His brow knitted down to emphasize his perplexed expression.

"I'm in love with her, Michael." The statement came out of his mouth as if he'd known it forever, as if the concept of being in love was the most comfortable thing in the world. Michael's eyes widened at his words. "Neither of us planned this situation. I swear to you. It started several weeks ago. I'm sure you don't want all the details. At first, I thought it would just be, you know…"

"One of your flings," Michael said, finishing his sentence. Mark flinched at the words. It bothered him that for the last few years, he'd used women for sexual gratification, and people he respected, like Michael, thought that may be all he was capable of.

"Yes." Mark bowed his head in shame momentarily. "But I want to take a chance on my relationship with her and I feel the best way to do that properly is to resign from the board."

"John and Elizabeth are in a relationship. He's remained on the board."

Mark nodded at Michael's point. "Yes. I've thought about that. But Elizabeth is much further removed from everything. Suzie is your executive assistant. She's entwined in all of the board meetings, the agenda, the minutes, and so forth. The ties between everyone are too close. Obviously, Seth Kriken picked up on it and is willing to exploit it." Mark scrubbed his hand down his face, trying to relax the tension that settled there. "What exactly did Kriken threaten?"

Michael huffed. "What didn't he? He said if we didn't remove you from the board immediately, he'd go public with your affair with Suzie. He said it wouldn't take much to plant the seeds of impropriety given Suzie's position with Advantage and your blatant display at the Beach Club. Plus, he warned me that he'd imply that I coerced Suzie to go after you in order to get an edge with the board on swing votes. It's absurd...I know. But we can't have him planting that sort of shit in the minds of others, no matter how ludicrous it sounds." Michael stood from behind his desk and motioned for Mark to follow him. He looked down at his watch. "Let's get in the board room. Everyone should be back from lunch by now. We'll open this discussion immediately instead of waiting until the end of the day."

"I wanted to be the one to bring this to your attention. I apologize. I thought the end of the day would be best. But when Seth met me at the dealership over lunch, I realized I should have just opened up the meeting with it this morning. Do you think this will go over well?" Mark stood and walked toward the door.

Michael swung an arm over his shoulder. "Nope. Not going to go over well at all. The guys aren't going to like to see you resign. I don't like seeing you resign, and John may want to go after this Kriken guy. You know what a hothead he can be." He chuckled as he escorted Mark out of the office and into the executive suite reception area.

Phillip Barker and Greg Snow stood at Suzie's desk chatting with her when Mark and Michael came around the corner.

"Let's round everyone up and get started," Michael said. "Suzie, there's been a slight change in the agenda. We need to not be disturbed for a while."

"Do you need me to change the agenda for the members?" she asked. Mark could hear the worry in her voice.

"No. We'll get to everything." Michael ushered Mark into the board room, but Mark could see the look of concern on Suzie's face. He wanted to say something to her, but perhaps it was better to deal with the board first.

****

"We can't just let this asshole start dictating how we handle situations," John Dorsey said. He slapped his hands on the board room table. "We give in to his demands, he's going to always think he has one over on us. What's next? He threatens to release this information if we don't make *him* a member of the board? I don't like it."

"John, we all understand your frustration," Phil said from the head of the table. Mark watched as John ran his fingers through his hair.

"Greg, isn't there some way to fight this asshole? Last I checked, blackmailing people wasn't exactly an ethical or legal maneuver."

Greg inhaled slowly in an obvious exercise to maintain his composure. Of all the guys on the board or that Mark knew, for that matter, Greg Snow was the most level-headed, but it was noticeable this topic was pushing even his patience. "We don't have to allow him to blackmail Mark, Suzie, or the company. There are certainly legal moves we can make to head him off at the forefront, but we don't have any control over what he puts out to the public. Of course, we can always go after him for slander after he opens his big mouth."

"Listen," Mark said. He rested his arms on the table. "Even before Seth made these threats, I was going to resign. Now it just makes even more sense. I appreciate all your support. You need to know that, but I think this is the best route for all of us and it keeps things from getting too messy."

"I don't fucking like it," John said again. "I get why you want to resign, Mark, I really do. But we can work around this situation with Suzie. There's got to be a way. You've got such great business insight. That's such an asset to this board."

"John is right," Phil said as he leaned back in the leather chair and crossed his arms over his chest. "We can find a way to work it out. We are willing to fight it out with this Seth character if need be."

"Gentlemen, I can't thank you enough," Mark said. His voice cracked as emotion welled in his chest at the outpour of support these men, his friends, were giving him. "But my mind is made up."

"Jesus Christ, Mark," John huffed. The exasperation overflowed from him. He pushed back in his chair and grasped the edge of the wooden table like he was going to catapult up and across the table at Mark. "I've got a flight to catch to Atlanta soon, and we still have two more issues to cover before the end of the session today. I'm not agreeing on this resignation. It doesn't settle right with me. Can we call a special meeting and further discuss this next week? Let's all sleep on it."

"I'm in agreement with John on this," Andy Price said. Mark looked at Andy, who was generally on the reserved side. The portly man settled back in the leather chair and folded his hands across his belly. "Sorry, Mark. I don't want to see you go."

"Guys, I've made my mind up. I planned to do this even before Seth Kriken's shenanigans."

"We need to carry on with the rest of today's agenda," Phil said. "We will tentatively accept your resignation, Mark. I'm going to ask Elizabeth to review the bylaws and see what the procedures are and we will get back together in a week to further discuss. I'll stop down in her office after the meeting today to discuss it with her. Michael will contact Seth and inform him of your resignation to keep him from going to the media with his ridiculous antics." Michael nodded his head. "Now, let's finish up today's business, so we can all start our weekend." Phil looked over at Mark and smiled. His eyes indicated the topic was closed for discussion, at least for today.

Chapter Eight

"They're still in there?" Suzie heard a familiar female voice say. She looked up from her computer where she typed out a few emails on behalf of her boss to see Elizabeth Wright waltzing into the executive suite. With her auburn hair tumbling over her shoulders and her navy blue pants suit conforming to her body, even Suzie's heart rate escalated whenever Elizabeth walked into the room. She was a knockout! And the kicker, she was sweeter than strawberry wine.

"Yep," Suzie said, smiling at Elizabeth. "They started a littler later than usual after lunch. Not sure what's going on in there."

Suzie replayed Mark storming through the executive suite doors after lunch with a murderous look on his face. He didn't reply at all to her inquires as to what was going on. Shortly thereafter, he and Michael rounded the board members up and ushered everyone into the board room asking not to be disturbed like some top secret CIA meeting. No one had been out of the board room for two hours, not even to use the restroom or refill the coffee.

"You here to see John?" Suzie asked as Elizabeth stood in front of Suzie's desk with her arms crossed over her chest.

"Yes! Darn it! I wanted to see him before he left. He's headed to Georgia today to check out a construction project outside of Atlanta. I won't get to see him until Monday." A frown spread across Elizabeth's mouth and her brow furrowed.

"I can send him down to your office as soon as he walks out," Suzie said, trying to help her out. Sure, Suzie had been shameless in her flirtations with John Dorsey.

John had even flirted with her a little too, but once Elizabeth walked into that board room to present to the board on some legal issues involving a lawsuit, John hadn't looked at another woman. Now they'd been living together for over eight months in John's beach house, and a little birdie had mentioned to Suzie that John was gearing up to ask her to marry him.

"That would be great. I have a couple things I need to wrap up before I can leave here. I think his flight is at five-thirty, so he's already cutting it close still being here after three," Elizabeth said with a little worry in her voice. "Thanks, Suzie." Elizabeth smiled at her and the smile reached her eyes, warmth emanating from her. Elizabeth turned and started toward the door when the board room door opened and John rushed out. His lips were pulled in a tight line, his brow was furrowed, and Suzie could tell he wasn't happy. Then he saw Elizabeth and his entire body relaxed, as if set at ease.

"Sweetheart," he said, flinging his bag over his shoulder and rushing in her direction. Elizabeth spun around.

"What's wrong, John?" she asked. Her own brow furrowed with worry when she saw him.

"Let's talk about it on the way downstairs," John said, his arms enveloping her. His lips came down on Elizabeth's, and Suzie felt as if she were imposing on a very private moment despite the fact that they stood just a few feet from where she sat working at her computer. After their slow kiss, John grabbed her hand and led her out of the executive suite, both of them oblivious to the world and deep in conversation.

Suzie dreamed of a relationship like that, and for brief little moments over the last week with Mark, she thought it might even be possible. But he'd barely said two words to her today. Even before they'd started having sex several weeks ago, he'd whispered sweet compliments in her ear that had shivers run down her spine. He'd stand at her desk for minutes on end talking about his daughters and trying to gain insight into the female mind, particularly the pre-teen female. After spending a week together, inseparable…today, nothing!

None of the other members exited the board room, so she went back to drafting a companywide email on Michael's behalf. What the hell could be keeping them so late today? Sitting still was becoming an impossibility. The energy emanating from Mark earlier and then John just now had her on edge.

What a glorious week it had been. She'd never been with a man that made her feel so alive. She yearned the whole eight hours at work for the end of the day just so she could see him again. Now, she didn't know what to think.

"Suzie." Mark's voice snapped her out of her reverie. She pushed to her feet, her chair rolling back. She winced as it slammed against the wall behind her. The board room doors stood wide open and the rest of the members were hustling about in the room.

"What is it?" she said. The panic in her voice was difficult to hide. "You're scaring the shit out of me." Her gaze met his, her heart pounding against her rib cage. He stepped closer to her and his hands cupped both sides of her face. Her eyes widened at his intimate contact, particularly in front of the others.

"I just resigned from the board," he said. His voice was so calm, she didn't think she heard him correctly.

"You what? Why?" Sadness bubbled to the surface and she couldn't stop her eyes from filling with tears. She'd been head over heels for this man for so long and she finally had a taste of what it was like to be with him. He was stripping her of any reason to have contact with him. Now she wouldn't even see him quarterly.

Jesus Christ! Did this past week mean nothing to him?

"Because I'm in love with you and I want to give us a chance," he said. Suzie's jaw dropped. She knew she must look ridiculous, her eyes wide, her mouth open, but he just said he loved her. "The best way for us to work is for me to separate myself from Advantage."

"But why?" she squeaked out. Her coherent thoughts were scattered and her mind wasn't capable of gathering them up at the moment. He just said he was in love with her.

"We'll talk about it later," he whispered. The warmth of his hands permeated her cheeks as he still cupped her face. "Right now, it's Friday, and I want to take you out on a proper date. In front of other people. Where I can show you off as my girlfriend, if you'll have me." Lowering his head, he pressed his lips gently to hers and, just like always, she melted into him. Her hands gripped his forearms for support as he kissed her thoroughly.

She didn't know how long she had stood there in the kiss with Mark before someone cleared his throat. Mark pulled back from their kiss and pulled her into his arms, nestling her close to his chest as he turned to look over his shoulder. His fresh masculine scent enveloped her and she breathed him in.

"Remember, Mark, this resignation is not yet permanent," Phil said. "We'll discuss it further next week."

"Not permanent? What's going on?" Suzie asked, tilting her head to the side to see the Chairman of the Board standing with his hands crossed over his chest in the doorway of the board room. The rest of group sans John stood behind him.

Turning his head back to her, Mark's thumb and forefinger gripped her chin and turned her head to look at him. "Seth Kriken was trying to make some trouble for me, for you, for Advantage. I don't want you to worry about anything, baby. I got this." Despite the desire to sink into him and let the excitement of his profession of love envelope her, she just couldn't get past the fact that he was leaving his position on the board for her.

"How am I not to worry? You're resigning, albeit it may not be permanent, from a position you love," she said. Lowering her voice, she said, "Is this because of me? Because of my sneaking into the bathroom at the Beach Club?" Her heart sank thinking that her actions gave this Seth creep ammunition against Mark…ammunition that had now cost him his position on the board—the thing he feared all along.

"Baby, it never had anything to do with you," he whispered. "Never. He's had it out for me since we went to high school together. Our parents were friends and I guess he's always felt like he was in my shadow. But even before he started this shit today, I was going to resign. I don't want anything to taint our attempt at a relationship."

He lowered his head and pressed his lips to hers again. She moaned softly, forgetting for a moment she was still standing behind her desk in the office until she heard the shuffle of the others. Her cheeks flushed and she pulled back from the kiss, burying her face in his chest.

"Don't stop on our account," Greg Snow said with a chuckle. Suzie turned her head slightly to see the burly attorney looking at her with his smiling grey eyes. Greg had always been one of the nicest men she'd ever met, always polite and concerned. "I'm happy for you." He winked at her before patting Mark on the back. "Touch base with me this coming week, buddy. We'll make some plans to golf, and the missus and I will have you guys over for dinner."

"Thanks, Greg," Mark said, smiling at his colleague and friend. "For everything."

"Any time." Greg patted his back one more time, gave Suzie's hand a squeeze, and stalked toward the executive doors. Over his shoulder, he said "Enjoy your weekend."

Several of the other board members issued warm sentiments their direction as they filed out of the executive suite to start their own weekends. Shaking her head just a little, she thought maybe she'd dreamt these whole last fifteen minutes, but she was still in Mark's arms.

"What is it, baby?" he asked softly next to her ear.

"I feel like I'm in a dream," she said. "I've been in love with you for so long, wanting so desperately for you to give me, give us, a chance. This past week was a peek into what we could be, but after the way you acted today, I thought maybe I was imagining everything. Now, you're telling me you love me. Is this a dream, Mark?"

"It's not a dream," he said. With his hand under her jaw, he tilted her face up to look into his eyes. His green eyes shone with emotion. "This is the start of our life." A tear slipped down the side of her cheek. Wiping the tear away with his thumb, he pressed his lips to hers.

Epilogue

"Let me see the ring." Suzie reached across the table and grabbed Elizabeth Wright's hand. Suzie and Mark had met their friends, John Dorsey, Elizabeth Wright, and Greg and Tessa Snow out for dinner and drinks at Bella Brava in downtown St. Petersburg. Being late in October, the weather was warm with a soft breeze hinting at the eventual Florida autumn, so they sat at a table on the outdoor patio facing Beach Drive and the Tampa Bay. The blue and pink streaked sky from the setting sun in the west cast a romantic hue as their backdrop.

On Elizabeth's left ring finger sat a beautiful princess cut diamond engagement ring. Looking up at her and then John Dorsey, who sat next to her, Suzie nodded her head. "Nice choice, John!"

"I know! Right?" Elizabeth squealed. Her eyes widened in delight, and the smile that spread across her lips could only be described as happiness. Suzie released her hand and Elizabeth stared at the ring on her finger for a few more seconds. "I didn't even drop him any hints as to what I liked or wanted, but he hit it perfectly. Not too big or gaudy. Simple. Classic. Perfect."

"She doesn't think she dropped any hints, but the longing looks every time we passed a jewelry store window gave her away." John laughed and slipped his arm around her shoulders, pulling her in for a hug. He pressed a soft kiss on her forehead, and Suzie melted at the sight of the two of them. She'd never witnessed such a perfect romance.

"Tell us how it happened," Tessa Snow said. "We want *all* the details." Suzie studied her other friend. She and Tessa had only known each other for a few months, but they were close in age and had come to find they had quite a bit in common. One of their commonalities was being in love with a man more than ten years their senior, who had each come with an ex-wife.

Tessa was glowing herself. Her blonde curls fell over her shoulders and her cheeks remained a rosy pink. Her gaze kept flipping over to her husband, Greg, who met her look each time with an endearing smile.

They'd gotten married less than six months after meeting last October. Suzie never believed such romances were smart, not knowing a person well enough before committing your life to them. Tessa and Greg dispelled that notion for her. Having known Greg for a few years as a member of the Advantage board, she'd always known he was a good guy...to the core. But the way he devoted himself to Tessa and their life together made Suzie's heart swell.

"The. Most. Romantic. Morning. Of. My. Life," Elizabeth said. Her face beamed with her glee and John laughed at her words.

"For a woman that I can never get to quit talking, that's quite a simple description of my proposal." He laughed again.

"Shut it, Dorsey," Elizabeth said, swatting at him. "I was just getting started." She cleared her throat and took a sip from her glass of pinot noir. "I was out on our deck last Sunday morning having my coffee. John was still sleeping, or so I thought. On weekends he has off, he usually sleeps late and I get my peace and quiet on the beach." She jabbed him with her elbow.

"Peace and quiet, eh? What are you implying?" He winked at her.

"That you like to hear yourself talk," Mark said with a laugh from across the table.

"Look who's talking," John shot back with a smile. The banter between the men always caused the girls to get giddy. It was like the guys were brothers, always picking on one another, yet always having each other's backs.

Neither John nor Greg took Mark's resignation lightly, both wanting to battle Seth Kriken so Mark could keep his place on the board. Mark would have none of it, though he did accept a consulting position on the board, which was just a quiet way for him to remain a part of the process without the formality of being an actual member. It didn't necessarily come with the same level of prestige or money, but Mark seemed more than happy with it.

Greg wrote a glaring letter to Seth, informing him that if he so much as breathed a word of his lies to the media or elsewhere, he would be slapped with a defamation and slander lawsuit before his story made the evening news. Suzie wasn't sure Mark knew about the letter Greg wrote because she had found out about it herself from Elizabeth, who pulled her aside at work the one day. Suzie never mentioned it to Mark because he seemed happy and she didn't want to ruin that for him.

"Will you two knock it off and let her finish the story? Sheesh!" Suzie said with exasperation as she slapped at Mark's arm.

"Thank you, Suzie." Elizabeth tossed her auburn hair over her shoulder and narrowed her eyes at her fiancé. "Anyway, unbeknownst to me, the whole time I was out on the deck reading a romance novel and enjoying my coffee, he was baking my favorite chocolate and peanut butter muffins. He came walking out with one on a plate and knelt next to the lounger. I didn't know what he was doing. First, he's not usually up at eight o'clock in the morning on his day off. Second, I knew I hadn't made the muffins so I was puzzled as to where they came from. Third, instead of sitting on the lounger next to me, he was kneeling. Ha! He was kneeling and it didn't even hit me."

"You bake, Dorsey?" Greg asked.

"That's what you're getting out of this story?" Tessa asked, a look of disbelief in her eyes.

"I knew the proposal was coming for weeks, Tess," Greg said. His grey eyes met Tessa's and something passed between the two of them that Suzie couldn't place. Tessa glanced over at Suzie and her cheeks flushed again at being caught in that moment with her husband. She grabbed her glass of water and took a sip before focusing her gaze back on Elizabeth. Suzie couldn't help but wonder what that was about. It was as if Tessa and Greg were keeping a secret.

"Go on," John encouraged Elizabeth.

"So, I asked him what he was doing."

"You actually said, 'What the fuck are you doing?'" John said with humor in his voice. Everyone at the table chuckled.

Elizabeth was attractive…to everyone. Her auburn hair, green eyes, and perfectly curved body turned heads everywhere. Even women looked at her with envy. She was sweet as sweet could be, and it often surprised people that she was a hard ass attorney with the occasional mouth of a sailor.

"This is my version and I was going to leave out the profanity, but since you already brought it up, yes, that is what I said." Her cheeks reddened, but she carried on. "So he said he made me my favorite muffins for breakfast and he held the plate out. On the top of the muffin was a toothpick with a cherry on top, a small ribbon, and this ring hanging from it." She held up her hand to display the gorgeous diamond again.

Tessa and Suzie squealed in unison with Elizabeth. Though the three of them hadn't been friends very long, it was clear to Suzie that these two women would always be dear to her heart.

"I think my mouth hung open and tears filled my eyes. And he said, 'Sweetheart, I've never been happier than this last year and a half with you. Will you be my wife?'" More squeals erupted around the table.

Several people from the two nearby tables turned to gape at them. "Sorry," Suzie said, waving her hand at the staring folks.

"Awww, Dorsey, I never knew you to be such a romantic," Mark teased. His hand rested on Suzie's knee and when she glanced at him, he gave it a gentle squeeze. She placed her hand over his and relished the feel of his skin against hers. To be able to be out in public with him as his girlfriend finally was a dream come true and she took every opportunity to appreciate their situation.

"I'm a softie when it comes to this woman." John leaned in and kissed her on the lips.

"He really is a softie," Elizabeth said after she caught her breath from his kiss. "He's tough on the outside, but it's all an act. I'm marrying a soft-hearted man."

"Sweetheart, you're going to ruin my reputation here," John said, smirking.

"I'm going to ruin you for the rest of your life, Mr. Dorsey," Elizabeth said with a glint of devilment in her eyes.

"Promises. Promises," John joked.

"Anyway, I couldn't stop the tears from pouring down my face," Elizabeth continued.

"But she said yes at least a hundred times," John said with a huge smile.

"That is true. And I think I've said it a hundred more times each day since." Elizabeth looked over at her fiancé, who picked up her hand from the table and kissed it. Just watching the two of them so in love with each other gave Suzie hope that she and Mark had a chance.

"Since we're on happy topics, Tess and I have something to share with you," Greg said. Tessa looked over at him with such adoration in her eyes. Suzie had noticed their sneaking glances at each other the entire time they'd been seated.

"Well, what is it?" Elizabeth asked. The impatience in her voice was impossible to disguise.

"Do you want to tell them?" Greg asked, looking at Tessa. She shook her head gently and smiled demurely at him. "Okay. Here goes. We're having a baby." Greg's voice was soft, but filled with delight.

"What?" the rest of the group shouted together. The people at the table next to them turned around again to see what all the fuss was about. All six of them burst into a brief fit of laughter.

"Tessa's pregnant," Greg said once he regained his composure. He made no effort to hide the smile that was plastered on his face.

"I was wondering why you were drinking water instead having some wine. How far along, Tess?" Suzie asked, winking at her friend.

"Yesterday was officially twelve weeks along, so I feel okay to share the news now. Plus, I'm almost over the morning, noon, and night sickness." She rubbed her hand over her belly, which actually still looked quite flat, but then again, Tessa was a lithe yoga instructor with hardly an ounce of fat on her body.

"Holy shit!" John Dorsey exclaimed. "You didn't even hint at this, Greg. Not even a hint." John shook his head in disbelief.

"I know," Mark said in agreement. "We just played golf two weekends ago and nothing! Not one clue!"

"Tessa wanted to keep quiet about it until we got beyond the first trimester. I promised her I wouldn't say anything." He looked over at her and smiled, nothing but devotion in his grey eyes.

"I didn't think he could do it," Tessa said, running her hand over Greg's forearm. "He's been bursting at the seams since I took the home pregnancy test and the plus sign showed up."

"What?" Greg said when all eyes trained on him. "I've always wanted to be a father. Tess has given me so much more than I ever thought possible."

Tessa leaned over in her chair and planted a smacking kiss on his cheek. "He's going to be an amazing dad!"

"That he is," Suzie said. "Oh God, I'm so happy for you guys. This is like the best night ever. Being here with all of you. Sharing in all this good news." She heard her voice crack and everyone's eyes softened when they looked at her, including Mark's.

"There's the sappy Suzie I love so much," Mark said, wrapping his arm around her neck and pulling her into him. He placed a kiss on her forehead and then tilted her chin up to kiss her lips softly. Everyone around the table "awed" at their public display of affection.

"Let's toast," John said, raising his glass of whiskey. Everyone around the table clasped their glasses and raised them toward the center of the table, including Tessa with her glass of water.

"To happy times," Elizabeth started. "To new beginnings."

"To good friends," Suzie said, smiling at everyone. Her heart was bursting with all sorts of emotions, being surrounded by two solid couples while she built her own relationship with an amazing man. She hadn't been this happy…ever.

The End

www.jessicajayneauthor.com

Evernight Publishing

www.evernightpublishing.com